PHINEAS L. MACGUIRE . . .
GETS COOKING!

Also by Frances O'Roark Dowell

Chicken Boy

Dovey Coe

Falling In

The Kind of Friends We Used to Be

Phineas L. MacGuire . . . Blasts Off!

Phineas L. MacGuire . . . Erupts!

Phineas L. MacGuire . . . Gets Slimed!

The Second Life of Abigail Walker

The Secret Language of Girls

Shooting the Moon

The Sound of Your Voice, Only Really Far Away

Ten Miles Past Normal

Where I'd Like to Be

PHINEAS L. MACGUIRE . . .

GETS COOKING!

by FRANCES O'ROARK DOWELL
illustrated by PRESTON McDANIELS

Atheneum Books for Young Readers
atheneum New York London Toronto Sydney New Delhi

ATHENEUM BOOKS FOR YOUNG READERS • An imprint of Simon & Schuster Children's Publishing Division • 1230 Avenue of the Americas, New York, New York 10020 • This book is a work of fiction. Any references to historical events, real people, or real places are used fictitiously. Other names, characters, places, and events are products of the author's imagination, and any resemblance to actual events or places or persons, living or dead, is entirely coincidental. • Text copyright © 2014 by Frances O'Roark Dowell • Illustrations copyright © 2014 by Preston McDaniels • All rights reserved, including the right of reproduction in whole or in part in any form. • ATHENEUM BOOKS FOR YOUNG READERS is a registered trademark of Simon & Schuster, Inc. • Atheneum logo is a trademark of Simon & Schuster, Inc. • For information about special discounts for bulk purchases, please contact Simon & Schuster Special Sales at 1-866-506-1949 or business@simonandschuster.com. • The Simon & Schuster Speakers Bureau can bring authors to your live event. For more information or to book an event, contact the Simon & Schuster Speakers Bureau at 1-866-248-3049 or visit our website at www.simonspeakers.com. • Also available in an Atheneum Books for Young Readers hardcover edition. • Book design by Sonia Chaghatzbanian • The text for this book is set in Garth Graphic. • The illustrations for this book are rendered in pencil. • Manufactured in the United States of America • 0916 OFF • First Atheneum Books for Young Readers paperback edition November 2015 • 10 9 8 7 6 5 4 3 2 • The Library of Congress has cataloged the hardcover edition as follows: • Dowell, Frances O'Roark. • Phineas L. MacGuire...gets cooking! / Frances O'Roark Dowell ; illustrated by Preston McDaniels.—First edition. • p. cm.—(From the highly scientific notebooks of Phineas L. MacGuire) • Summary: "Phineas has a new chore of cooking dinner every night, but his kitchen experiments take a turn for the worse when the school bully takes a huge liking to Phineas's brownies"—Provided by publisher. • ISBN 978-1-4814-0099-2 (hc) • ISBN 978-1-4814-0100-5 (pbk) • ISBN 978-1-4814-0101-2 (eBook) • [1. Cooking—Fiction. 2. Science—Experiments—Fiction. 3. Bullying—Fiction. 4. Schools—Fiction. 5. Friendship—Fiction.] I. McDaniels, Preston, illustrator. II. Title. • PZ7.D75455Phg 2014 • [Fic]—dc23 • 2014008463

For Win Hill and Gavin Schulz,
two of my favorite geniuses

PHINEAS L. MACGUIRE . . .

GETS COOKING!

chapter one

My name is Phineas L. MacGuire.
A few people call me Phineas, but
most people call me Mac. Yesterday,
when I was riding the bus to school, I
came up with a bunch of cool things
the *L* in my name could stand for. My
list included:

1. Lithosphere (the outmost shell
   of a rocky planet)
2. Lunar Eclipse

3. Light-Year
4. Labrador Whisperer

Unfortunately, the *L* in my name does not stand for any of those things. It stands for Listerman, which was, like, my mom's great-aunt Tulip's last name or something. My mom is very big on family traditions, but even she's not allowed to call me Listerman.

I mean, ever.

You can probably tell by the first three things on my list of *L* names that I am a scientist. In fact, I'm the best fourth-grade scientist at Woodbrook Elementary School. Or at least sort of the best. There's this girl in my class named Aretha Timmons who might be kind of as good at science as I am, but her goal is not to be the greatest scientist in the whole world one day, which mine is. I think that gives me the edge.

The last thing on my list has to do with a certain Labrador retriever named Lemon Drop. I walk Lemon Drop every day after school, and earlier this year I did a major dog slobber experiment inspired by Lemon Drop's natural dog slobberiness. It was awesome.

The fourth grade has been my best year as a scientist ever. So far I have:

1. Gotten an honorable mention in the fourth-grade science fair.
2. Grown my own slime

and established the Phineas L. MacGuire Mold Museum in my bedroom.

3. Performed important dog slobber experiments that prove, when you get down to it, slobber is alive.

4. Attended Space Camp and ridden the Mars roller coaster without throwing up.

For most people, that would be enough for one year, but when you're a scientist like me, you want to do scientific stuff all the time.

The problem is, sometimes you run out of good ideas.

I've been in the middle of a serious dry spell that has lasted over two weeks, and I've been feeling pretty grumpy about it. Usually I'm in a good mood, so people notice when I'm not. Yesterday

my teacher, Mrs. Tuttle, put one of the rubber frogs from the jar she keeps on her desk on top of my head. She was trying to make me laugh.

Everybody else laughed, but I didn't.

At lunch my best friend, Ben Robbins, who is a genius artist, drew a bunch of pictures of me as a superhero scientist. There was one where I was wearing a lab coat and holding up an exploding beaker of chemicals. It was really cool-looking, but it didn't cheer me up.

During recess Aretha went out and found three dried worms to give me for my dried worm collection. This should have made me extremely happy, since this hasn't been a good spring for dried worms, and I'm behind on my monthly quota. And it sort of did make me happy, but only for about ten minutes.

Then I went back to feeling grumpy because I didn't have a good science project to do.

My mom has been grumpy a lot lately too. She's a naturally irritable person, but that's not the same thing as being grumpy. Being irritated is a reaction to a situation. Being grumpy is a state of mind.

"I don't know why I can't lose this last five pounds," she complained at dinner last night. She took another bite of pizza before saying, "Phyllis and I walk two miles every day on our lunch break. You'd think the pounds would just fall off."

My stepdad, Lyle, reached across the table and grabbed a slice from the box. "You look great, Liz. I'm glad you're exercising, but you don't need to do it to lose weight."

"We could stop eating pizza all the time," I said. "That might help."

I should point out that I wasn't actually eating pizza. Pizza is pretty much my favorite food group, but I've learned you can get tired of even stuff you love a lot if you have to eat it three nights a week. So for the second night in a row I was eating a bowl of Cheerios for dinner.

My mom's expression was 50 percent grumpy and 50 percent irritated. "Mac, we've been through this. I'm tired when I get home after a long day at work. So's

Lyle. Cooking takes time, and it takes energy, two things I really don't have a lot of at the end of the day."

I shrugged. "I'm just saying that scientifically speaking, it's hard to lose weight when all you eat is pizza. I'm not complaining or anything."

"You might be complaining just a little bit, and I guess I don't blame you," my mom said, and then she smiled a grumpy sort of smile. "I can't tell you how often I wished the workday was like a school day—you know, home by three, plenty of time to get everything done. If I got home at three every day, I'd be able to—"

She paused. She looked at me for what seemed like a really long time. And then she got this smile on her face. A very scary kind of smile.

"I know just what to do about it," my mom said, picking up her phone and tapping on the keyboard. After she was done, she said, "There! Problem solved!"

Lyle and I looked at each other like, *What's going on?*

My mom lost her grumpy expression. In fact, she looked downright happy. That sort of scared me, if you want to know the truth.

"I've just texted Sarah that tomorrow when you get home from school, she's to take you to the grocery store."

By Sarah, she means my babysitter from outer space. Going anywhere with Sarah was not high on my list of things to do.

"Why?" I asked.

My mom smiled. "Because from now on, you're going to cook dinner, Mac. And I know you'll do an amazing job."

chapter two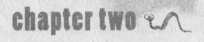

"Wait, you have to do all the cooking from now on?" Ben shook his head, then swung his way across the monkey bars. "That's, like, a mega amount of work, Mac," he said when he reached the other side. "You won't have time to do anything else."

"I just have to make dinner," I

told him. "Lyle's still going to make our lunches, and we're all sort of on our own for breakfast."

"Even Margaret?"

Margaret is my two-year-old sister. "No, my mom fixes her breakfast. Only Margaret never eats it. She just mushes up the toast and the banana and smears it all over her face."

Ben grimaced. "Little kids are so gross."

"It's actually sort of cool-looking," I told him, grabbing on to the first bar of the monkey bars and swinging back and forth. "Like slime mold."

As far as I'm concerned, there is nothing cooler in the world than a little bit of slime.

"But I don't get how you're going to do dinner all by yourself," Ben said, starting to draw a picture in the dirt with a stick. "You're not even ten yet. That's kinda young to be in charge of the most important meal of the day."

"I thought breakfast was the most important meal of the day."

"Yeah, that's what Mrs. Tuttle says, but here's my question: Do you have dessert with breakfast?"

I shook my head.

"I rest my case," Ben said, taking a bow. "You can have dessert with lunch, it's true, but usually it's a pretty small dessert, like a couple of cookies or something. But dessert after dinner? We're talking ice cream, my friend, we're talking cake, pie, baked Alaska."

"You have baked Alaska for dessert?"

"Theoretically speaking, I could," Ben said. "I'm not actually sure what baked Alaska is, to be honest, but I know nobody ever has it after they've eaten breakfast."

I didn't know anybody who ate dessert after breakfast, though I did know a few people who sort of ate dessert *for* breakfast. There's this kid in our class, Roland Forth, who gets on the bus every morning carrying a doughnut wrapped in a napkin. Some days it's a powdered doughnut, other days it's one with sprinkles. Everybody around him says, "Hey, Roland, I'll be your best friend if you give me half," or "Hey, Roland, if you give me your doughnut, I'll do your homework," but Roland never shares. He just sits and eats and makes these little happy humming noises.

Roland Forth is a famous hummer, in case you were wondering. It's like having a radio playing in your class all day long.

In case you're wondering, Roland Forth is also pretty annoying.

I sat down next to Ben in the dirt and started collecting pebbles to make a frame for the picture he was drawing. "My mom thinks making me cook dinner is the greatest idea in the world, but it's pretty stupid, if you ask me. First of all, I don't know anything about cooking. I mean, okay, I can use the toaster oven to heat up frozen waffles, but that's it. And when I told my mom I don't know how to cook, she said that Sarah can teach me."

Ben's eyes widened. "Whoa! That's harsh."

Totally harsh. Time with Sarah is not time well spent, in my book. She is seriously into purple, a color I happen to be allergic to, and she is always trying to make me eat nutritious snacks after school. I would find her 100 percent annoying except for the fact that she built a mold museum in my room earlier this year and found twelve dried worms for my collection.

You have to admit, it's hard to be 100 percent annoyed by a babysitter who understands your passion for mold.

Still, spending my afternoons cooking with Sarah did not sound like a great plan to me. It sounded more like a punishment.

"And anyway," I told Ben, "cooking seems totally boring. Besides, it's really more of a girl thing than a boy thing."

"Excuse me, did I just hear you say cooking is a girl thing?"

I looked up to see Aretha Timmons standing behind me. Uh-oh. Aretha definitely didn't like it when you said only boys can do this and only girls can do that. Come to think of it, Ben didn't either, since he wanted to be an artist and his dad said that art was for girls.

"Well, y-you know," I stammered, "it just seems like something girls, uh, sort of like more than boys. I mean, Melissa Beamer and Michelle Lee are always talking about baking cupcakes, and Stacey Windham watches every show on the Cooking Channel."

Aretha put her hands on her hips. "And you think that means cooking is a girl thing? Just because you know three girls who cook? Well, I can name at least three guys who cook, number one being my dad. He cooks dinner every night."

Come to think of it, my dad

cooks a lot too. I go stay with him every other weekend, and he makes these big pans of lasagna and baked ziti. In fact, he's a much better cook than my mom, except when it comes to pumpkin pie. My mom is, like, the world's best pumpkin pie maker. It's one of her most stellar qualities, besides the fact she totally gets that I'm a serious scientist, which not every mom of a fourth grader would.

Aretha raised three fingers. She tapped one and said, "Okay, so number one guy cook is my dad, and"—she tapped another finger—"number two is my grandfather, who taught my dad to cook in the first place. Number three is Mr. Reid. You know those awesome chocolate-chip cookies at the bake sales? Mr. Reid!"

Mr. Reid is our school janitor and a fellow scientist. I didn't know he was a baker, too. "I thought Mrs. Reid made those cookies," I said.

Aretha shook her head. "Mac, Mac, Mac. Welcome to the twenty-first century. *Everybody* cooks. Besides, I thought you'd be into cooking."

I stood up and wiped the dirt from my jeans. "Why?!"

"Because cooking is science," Aretha said. "It's chemistry!"

Ben drew a huge atomic cloud in the dirt. "Even I knew that!" he said.

Chemistry? I thought about scientists in lab coats wearing protective goggles and gloves and pouring dangerous chemical concoctions into beakers, watching as purple-and-blue smoke poured out. I thought about the chemistry set my mom wouldn't let me get because she thought I'd burn a huge hole in the kitchen floor with the chemicals.

When I thought about chemistry, I never once thought about cooking.

But now I could sort of see it.

"I need to go do some research," I told Aretha and Ben. "When's recess over?"

Aretha checked her totally awesome watch, which doesn't just tell the time, it gives you the weather report too. "Ten minutes," she informed me.

That was just enough time to get started. I ran to the library and got permission from Mrs. Rosen, our school librarian, to use the computer. I searched "chemicals used in cooking," and this is the list I made:

1. Baking soda, also known as $NaHCO_3$ or sodium bicarbonate
2. Salt, also known as NaCl or sodium chloride
3. Baking powder, a mix of cream

of tartar and sodium bicarbonate
4. Cream of tartar, which is potassium bitartrate, also called potassium hydrogen tartrate
5. Lemon juice, also known as citric acid, also known as $C_6H_8O_7$

Here's what else I discovered. There's a kind of science that's all about experimenting with chemistry

in cooking. You can go to college to study it, and even get your PhD.

In other words, I wouldn't just be a cook, I'd be a molecular gastronomist.

That, I liked the sound of.

chapter three

Going to the grocery store with Sarah Fortemeyer is not my idea of fun. In fact, I try to avoid doing anything with Sarah if at all possible. My Sarah Fortemeyer phobia began last year, when she first started babysitting us and asked if she could paint my fingernails. She was testing out different colors, and she'd already painted her nails and Margaret's.

I'd run upstairs as fast as I could and

shoved a chair against my door. Ever since then I've avoided Sarah Fortemeyer like two weeks' worth of extra homework whenever possible.

But today she wasn't so bad. First of all, she wasn't armed with fingernail polish. Then, she actually let me do the shopping by myself while she and Margaret looked at magazines. "Pasta's on aisle two, and so is the spaghetti sauce," she told me, handing me the list. "Your mom says to get the organic kind. Frozen garlic bread's in the frozen food section, and the bagged salad is over in produce."

I have to admit, it didn't sound like the most scientific dinner in the world. Where was the baking soda? The citric acid? Tonight's dinner was strictly amateur stuff. Normally this would be okay, since I'm a kid, but I'm also a scientist.

As a scientist, I was hoping for the kind of dinner that might blow up at the last minute.

I pushed the cart to aisle two. Was there a science to cooking spaghetti? I wondered. Why did the water need to be boiling to cook pasta? Why couldn't you just soak the pasta in cold water? Would it still get soft?

When I got to the shelves where all the pasta was, I could see it wasn't going to be as simple as just grabbing a box and chucking it into the cart. If my calculations were correct, there were seventeen different kinds of spaghetti, including thin spaghetti, regular spaghetti, whole wheat spaghetti, pasta-plus spaghetti,

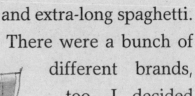 and extra-long spaghetti. There were a bunch of different brands, too. I decided to get the box that looked most familiar, but I got the extra-large size, because I wasn't sure how much spaghetti I needed to cook for four people. I read the instructions on the back of the box, which said a serving was two ounces, but that didn't seem like enough to me. Besides, better too much than not enough, right?

There were even more kinds of spaghetti sauce than spaghetti, but there were only two kinds of organic sauce, which made choosing a lot easier. I got the kind that cost eight dollars instead of the kind that cost four dollars, because I figured the eight-dollar stuff would be twice as good.

"Wow, pretty fancy," Sarah said when I showed her everything I'd gotten. "Are you sure your mom wants you to spend that much on the sauce?"

"She only wants the best for her family," I assured Sarah.

"Okay," Sarah said with a shrug. "Let's get this stuff home and start cooking."

When I walked into the kitchen, I decided to think of it as my lab. The stove was a giant Bunsen burner, and the pots and pans were beakers and flasks. *If only I had a lab coat,* I thought, and then I had a brilliant idea. I ran upstairs and grabbed one of Lyle's white work shirts. It was long enough on me to look like a coat. All I had to do was roll up the sleeves a million times and I looked like a genius scientist. If I did say so myself.

Next, I needed a plan. When you work in a lab, you have to be organized. I read the instructions on the pasta box, which said that I should boil the spaghetti for ten to twelve minutes. I started to write that down on the notepad my mom leaves on the counter, but then I stopped. Ten minutes didn't seem long enough for two pounds of pasta. I checked out the serving size, which was two ounces. If you multiply two ounces by four servings, you get eight ounces, or a half-pound. But since I was going to make two pounds of spaghetti so we could have leftovers the next night, I calculated I should boil the pasta for four times as long: forty to forty-eight minutes.

Easy peasy.

I got out a big pot from the cabinet, filled it up with water, and then put it on the burner. Here's where I ran into my first problem.

I'm not allowed to use the stove.

"Hey, Sarah!" I called. "How am I supposed to cook dinner if turning on the stove is against the rules?"

Sarah came in from the living room, where she'd been having a tea party with Margaret. "Do you know how to turn it on?"

I felt my face turn red. "Uh, not really."

"No need to be embarrassed, little buddy," Sarah said, patting me on the shoulder, which made me feel even more embarrassed. "There's a first time for everything."

Then she showed me what I needed to do. We have a gas stove, which is pretty cool, because you have to get the gas going and then twist the knob to just the right place. *Swoosh!* A flame pops up and you're ready to cook!

The instructions on the pasta box said I had to let the water come to a boil before I put the spaghetti in the pot. I didn't know how long that would take,

so I thought I'd go ahead and pour the sauce into another pan and start heating that up. Which is where I ran into my second problem.

I couldn't get the lid off the jar.

"Like I said, there's a first time for everything, right?" Sarah said, patting me on the back again. "The trick to this is use a rubber glove. It gives you more traction, which, in case you're wondering, is just another word for adhesive force."

I hadn't been wondering, actually, but it was good to know.

Sarah wrapped the lid with one of the yellow rubber gloves by the sink, took a deep breath, and twisted. The top popped off.

"Know why the jar makes that popping sound when it comes off?" Sarah asked.

"Um, I'm not sure," I said, my face getting even redder. I was starting to feel like a total failurezoid in the lab. "Maybe it's gas that's being released from the jar? Maybe the contents are under pressure, and then you open the lid and everything rushes out?"

Sarah nodded. "That sounds like a good explanation. Hey, do you know how to turn on the oven? You need to start preheating it for the garlic bread."

That, I did know.

Five minutes later I had the sauce heating up in a pot, the garlic bread unwrapped and on a baking tray, and the box of spaghetti ready to dump in the water, just as soon as the water started to boil.

I also had six spaghetti sauce stains on Lyle's shirt, but I was pretty sure they'd wash out.

Then a couple of things happened all at once. One, my mom got home from work. Two, Sarah started giving her the daily report. Three, the water came to a boiling point, which means, in case you're wondering, that it had reached a temperature of 212 degrees Fahrenheit.

So while my mom and Sarah were talking, I dumped the spaghetti into the pot. All two pounds of it.

That might not have been the greatest idea in the world.

After dinner was over, I decided to write a lab report, which is what scientists do, whether their experiments are successful or not. I wrote down the name of the experiment, the steps I had taken, and the results. Finally, I wrote down a list of everything I'd learned, including:

1. After you put spaghetti in boiling water, you need to stir it.

Otherwise, it all clumps together into one big pasta log.

2. It's also a good idea to stir your spaghetti sauce if you don't want most of it to burn to the bottom of the pot.

3. Two pounds of pasta is enough to feed a family of four for about a week.
4. When you cook pasta for forty minutes, it sort of disintegrates. Forget about eating it. I mean, just totally forget about it.
5. Cheerios for dinner is really pretty good, especially with garlic bread.

chapter four

I spent lunch today reading this book my mom gave me called *The Joy of Cooking*. After last night's dinner disaster, I thought I'd be kicked off kitchen duty, but my mom says every cook makes mistakes, especially at the beginning, and the only way to learn is to try, try again.

Actually, my mom was pretty nice about me ruining dinner. The only thing that made her mad was me wearing Lyle's shirt. She was a little bit irritated because I got spaghetti sauce on it, and slightly more irritated that I'd spent eight bucks on the sauce in the first place, but she was super mad because wearing oversize clothing—especially a big shirt with long sleeves—in the kitchen is dangerous.

"Safety in the lab is a scientist's number one priority," she told me. "So tomorrow night, wear a T-shirt."

At lunch, I was reading the chapter called "Know Your Ingredients" when Ben practically skidded into the chair next to me.

"Fantastizoid news, Mac!" he exclaimed, smacking a piece of paper on top of my book. "Your great cooking experiment could not come at a better time! Just look at this contest we're going to win!"

I glanced at the piece of paper, which

looked like it had been torn out of a magazine. THE COOKING CHANNEL'S FIRST ANNUAL RECIPE CONTEST! the headline shouted up at me in superbright yellow letters. ENTER AND WIN $10,000, PLUS A BRAND-NEW KITCHEN!

"What do I need a brand-new kitchen for?" I asked, pushing the announcement back toward Ben. "I've already got a kitchen."

Ben shook his head. "It's not the kitchen we're after, Mac. It's the money! Ten thousand buckaroos! We'll split it fifty-fifty and each still have a load of dough. Me, I'm using my half to go to Hawaii and learn how to surf."

Ben's big dream has always been to be a rock star surfboarder. Well, his *big* big dream is to be a famous cartoonist, and he thinks surfing is a part of the cartoonist lifestyle.

I have no idea where he comes up with this stuff.

"Okay, so the money would be nice," I said. "The only problem is, I'm just learning how to cook, and you don't know how to cook at all. So how are we supposed to come up with some award-winning recipe?"

"We'll spend this weekend having a Cooking Channel marathon at my apartment," Ben said, sounding confident. "We'll pick up all sorts of useful information, some good cooking tips and what have you, and by Sunday we'll figure out a great recipe. According to the announcement, we have to e-mail our recipe, preferably with pics of the finished product, by Monday, April 8. That gives us two and a half weeks."

Suddenly, there was a loud popping noise to my left. I turned and saw Aretha popping her pencil against the table. At our school, fourth-grade boys and girls don't sit together at lunch, even when they're fellow scientists. If you do, people will automatically start calling you boyfriend and girlfriend.

I try to avoid that at all costs, and so does Aretha. So what we usually do at lunch is sit at tables next to each other, in case we have any important scientific information to share.

Aretha had her *Girl Scout Handbook* open in front of her, but she was looking straight at me. "Two weeks isn't much time, Mac. The good news is you're in luck. I've just started working on a cooking badge, and helping you would help me."

"But I don't really know how to cook," I repeated. "I think it would help to know how to actually cook stuff if I wanted to make up my own recipe."

"Yeah, which is where my great idea comes in," Aretha said. "See, I've got to do this unit on eggs to get my badge. My dad's going to teach me how to cook eggs on Saturday, and it would be a lot more fun if you

and Ben were there. I bet my dad would give us all kinds of helpful cooking hints. Plus, I've got to make up an egg recipe and come up with a food science project. So we can brainstorm together. Three brains are better than one." She glanced at Ben. "Or two brains. Whatever."

Aretha started packing up her lunch bag. "The thing about coming up with recipes is, you don't have to be totally original. Think of something you really love to eat, and then imagine ways you could make it better."

"Right!" Ben exclaimed. "Like me, personally, I love a banana–peanut butter smoothie. And you know what would make that even more better? Bacon. See! I'm a genius! We've got this contest in the bag."

"You think you're going to win with a

banana, peanut butter, and bacon smoothie?" I asked.

"You think I should throw some strawberry jelly in there too?"

Aretha and I looked at each other. Then we looked at Ben.

Then we both yelled "No!" so loud that everybody in the cafeteria turned around and looked at us.

Ben shrugged. "It was just an idea."

"So what are you going to cook for dinner tonight, Mac?" Aretha asked, closing her *Girl Scout Handbook*. It was almost time to go out to the playground for recess.

"My mom said maybe I should try something simple, like homemade waffles. Which would be good, since we've got all the ingredients."

"I love breakfast for dinner!" Ben said. "As long as you still get real dessert, that is."

I lugged *The Joy of Cooking* out with me to the playground. I was pretending it was a chemistry textbook, which it sort of was, although it probably had more oatmeal cookie recipes than your average chemistry textbook. While Ben went to play soccer with a bunch of third graders, I sat down on the stairs by the door and got back to reading about ingredients.

It was actually a lot more interesting than you might think.

For instance, I learned that yeast cells reproduce really fast if you give them some warm water and sugar. It turns out that water and sugar are to yeast what chocolate-chip ice cream is to human beings.

While the cells are growing and reproducing, they produce these things called enzymes. When I looked this up in the dictionary later, I learned that enzymes are catalysts for chemical reactions. In other words, enzymes are the movers and shakers of the chemical world. The enzymes produced by the yeast convert starch into sugar. The yeast eats the sugar and then produces carbon dioxide gas, and that's what makes the dough get all puffy.

YEAST

To put it another way, it's kind of like the yeast ate a bunch of junk food and farted.

But in a good way.

I was just starting to get into the section on baking powder and biscuits when a shadow fell over the page. I looked up and saw Evan Forbes. As always, he was wearing red Chucks, a gray hoodie, and a blue-and-red-striped T-shirt. It was sort of his uniform. He kicked up some dust with one of his Chucks and sneered at me.

I knew that whatever happened next, it would not be good.

I've never understood kids like Evan Forbes. For one thing, it seems like he lives to make other kids unhappy. For another thing, he never does his homework. Just today, Mrs. Tuttle dismissed us for lunch but told Evan to wait. I was

the last one out of the classroom, so I overheard her say, "I'm going to have to call your parents, Evan. This is the third time this week you haven't turned in your math assignment."

"Go ahead," Evan had answered in a loud voice, like he didn't care if anybody heard. "My parents say it's my choice. If I don't feel like doing homework, I don't have to."

Yeah, right, I thought. I glanced back over my shoulder, expecting to see Evan looking all tough and mean, but to my surprise he sort of looked like he was about to cry.

It was pretty weird, if you want to know the truth.

"Hey, Mr. Top Chef!" Evan said, reaching down and flipping my book shut. "I thought you were some hotshot scientist or something, but I guess I was wrong about that. It turns out you're a culinary artist!"

Actually, I was kind of impressed by Evan's vocabulary. "Culinary" was a pretty advanced word for a Neanderthal like him.

"I *am* a scientist," I told him. "Have you ever heard of something called a molecular gastronomist?"

"I've heard of a chowderhead," Evan said. "That's what you look like to me."

"I don't know how to make chowder yet," I said. I was trying to make a joke, but my voice came out sort of squeaky. "Besides, I think I might be allergic to clams. I'm allergic to a lot of stuff."

Have I mentioned that I'm allergic to fifteen things, including avocados, cottage cheese, grape jelly, celery, and anything purple? My mom says that the only things I'm actually allergic to are peanuts and cat hair, but I have documented proof that purple ink gives me hives.

Evan shook his head. "I oughta clobber you. But, listen, I'm gonna give you a break. My sources tell me you're all into this cooking thing now, and I could really use some brownies. My mom's on this health kick, and sugar's, like, against the law in my house. I haven't had a brownie in two weeks. So here's the deal—you make me some brownies, and I'll let you live a little while longer."

"Why don't you just go to the store and buy some brownies?" I asked.

Evan shook his head. "Store-bought brownies aren't the same as homemade. Not even in the same universe. So meet me here tomorrow before school with a dozen brownies in an unmarked paper bag. That is, if you're interested in keeping all your teeth."

I watched Evan walk across the playground and join a game of football. It was supposed to be touch football, but every time the playground monitor turned her back, somebody got tackled. I mean, tackled as in thrown down to the ground and trampled on.

Scientifically speaking, I was in big trouble.

chapter five

There were a few minutes left in recess, so I ran down to Mr. Reid's office. Maybe he could give me some helpful hints for baking brownies.

"The best recipe I know is in that book you're holding right there," Mr. Reid told me. "Let's take a look, and I'll walk you through it."

Mr. Reid pulled up a chair next to his desk, and we both sat down. "So when do you want to make these brownies?"

he asked, searching the *The Joy of Cooking*'s index for the recipe.

"As soon as possible," I told him. I didn't mention that my life might depend on it. "The minute I get home from school."

"Do you know if you've got what you need?" He found the brownie recipe page and ran his finger down the list of ingredients. "Do you have butter and eggs?"

I nodded.

"Flour and sugar?"

I nodded again.

"Four ounces of unsweetened baking chocolate?"

This time I shook my head. "I'm pretty sure we have chocolate chips. Could I just use those?"

"Nope, because the recipe already has sugar in it, you see. But no worries—I always keep a few baking supplies in my drawer here." Mr. Reid pulled out his bottom desk drawer, and I could see that he wasn't kidding. There were plastic containers marked FLOUR and SUGAR and boxes of salt, baking powder, and baking soda. At the very back was a box labeled BAKING CHOCOLATE.

"Sometimes, if one of the teachers is having a bad day, I take my ingredients up to the kitchen and bake 'em something. I'm pretty famous around here for my brownies, as a matter of fact."

Mr. Reid shook four little blocks of chocolate wrapped in wax paper out of the box and handed them to me. "Now, the tricky thing about chocolate is that it burns really easily when you melt it. So what you have to do is chop it up and put it in a microwave-safe bowl with the butter, which you need to cut up into cubes. Microwave it for forty-five seconds, stir, and microwave it again—but only for forty-five seconds. Let it sit a minute, then microwave it for maybe thirty seconds."

"Why does chocolate burn so easily?"

"Low melting temperature," Mr. Reid explained. "It melts in your mouth, right? So let's say it melts at ninety degrees. Heat it up much higher than that, the cocoa butter separates from the solids and everything burns up. It's not pretty."

"I wonder why things have different melting points," I said. "I mean, all liquids have the same boiling point, right? And everything freezes at the same point, when they get below thirty-two degrees."

"Actually, Mac, only water freezes at thirty-two degrees," Mr. Reid told me. "Everything has its own freezing point, which is usually the same as its melting point. It just depends on whether something's moving toward the state of becoming a solid or becoming a liquid."

I must have looked as confused as I felt, because Mr. Reid smiled and said,

"Just think about a piece of ice, Mac. Ice is frozen water. Freezes at thirty-two degrees Fahrenheit, right? So when does that piece of ice start to melt?"

I thought about it for a minute and then made a guess. "Eighty degrees?"

Mr. Reid shook his head. "Way too high, Mac. Now, this might twist your brain into a knot, but the melting point of ice and the freezing point of ice are exactly the same. It's called being in equilibrium. So water freezes at thirty-two degrees, but ice can be considered to be melting at thirty-two degrees. If chocolate melts at ninety degrees, it also is starting to freeze at ninety degrees."

You know the weird thing? I almost understood what Mr. Reid was saying.

Almost.

But not really.

"Okay, enough about thermodynamics," Mr. Reid said, looking at his watch. "You should be back in your classroom. Do you have any more questions about brownies? You can always call me at home later. Just follow the instructions, Mac. Cooking is chemistry, right?"

"Right." I nodded, trying to look confident. All I knew for sure was that if I burned the chocolate, I couldn't make the brownies, and if I didn't make brownies, I was a goner.

When Ben heard I was making brownies, he immediately wanted to help. "This could be like practice for when we come up with our prizewinning recipe. We could mix stuff in the brownie batter—you know, experiment. We could mix in bacon!"

"You're obsessed with bacon," I told him. "Bacon in brownies, bacon in milk shakes. Bacon's not even healthy."

"My mom says that nitrate-free bacon isn't so bad." Ben lowered his voice to a whisper, since Mrs. Tuttle was giving us the evil eye for talking during silent reading period. "The fact is, Mac, bacon just makes everything better. That's sort of my motto."

"Well, I'm not putting bacon in these brownies," I whispered back. "And I'm— I'm not allowed to have anyone over today. You know, since I messed up Lyle's shirt and everything."

"Bummer," Ben whispered. "Maybe tomorrow?"

"Maybe," I said, and then I pointed to the book on my desk, like we better start reading before Mrs. Tuttle got really mad and started throwing frogs at us.

I hated lying to Ben about not being able to come over, but I knew if he helped me make the brownies, he'd end up eating at least half of them, and then Evan Forbes would halfway kill me. Which maybe was better than being all the way killed, but not much.

When I got home, Sarah and Margaret were playing beauty parlor in the kitchen. "Hey, Mac, have a snack attack!" Sarah called out when I walked in. "There's some yogurt in the fridge."

"I'm allergic to yogurt," I reminded her, dropping my backpack by the door. "All flavors."

"Your mom says you're not," Sarah said, smearing some raspberry-colored lipstick on Margaret's lips. "And she says you need more protein in your diet. Yogurt's perfect."

"Except for the fact that I'd probably go into anaphylactic shock the minute I ate some," I told her.

"That's what happens with peanuts, Mac. Not yogurt."

"Anyway, I don't have time for a snack," I said. "I need to get cooking. I've got brownies to make."

Margaret clapped her hands. "Brownies! Yum!"

"Sorry, Margaret, they're for school. I'll make you some tomorrow."

"Wow, you're really getting into

this baking thing, huh?" Sarah pulled Margaret toward her so she could put red stuff on her cheeks. "It makes sense, I guess."

"Why? Because cooking is chemistry, and I'm a scientist?"

Sarah smiled. "That, plus chicks dig a guy who bakes."

I could feel the hives popping up across my back. Have I mentioned that I'm allergic to girls, too?

Well, I am.

I was super careful to follow the recipe. All I had was the chocolate that Mr. Reid gave me, so I couldn't mess up. I chopped up the chocolate and put it in a microwave-safe bowl with the butter, and I did exactly what Mr. Reid had told me to. To my major-zoid happiness, the chocolate melted without burning.

And it smelled better than anything in the world.

How did it taste before I mixed in the sugar?

You don't want to know.

Neither my mom nor Lyle do much baking, so I wasn't prepared for the amazing smells that came out of the oven. In fact, they smelled so good, I had to call my dad and tell him about them.

"Best smell in the world," he agreed. I could hear his team behind him, yelling and joking around. My dad teaches high school math and coaches the Mathlete team after school. "In fact, when you're here next weekend, let's make some."

"I'll be an expert by then," I told him. "And this weekend I'm going over to Aretha's to make eggs. She's working

on a cooking badge for Girl Scouts."

"Great! You can make omelets for breakfast!" A loud burst of noise erupted through the phone. "Whoops, gotta run—we've got a totally out-of-control quadratic equation situation going on here."

I hung up the phone and breathed in some more of that great brownie smell. When the timer went off, I pulled the brownies out of the oven. They looked perfect. They smelled perfect.

And okay, they tasted perfect too.

I mean, I couldn't give Evan Forbes brownies that hadn't been through a taste test, could I?

The only problem was, after the brownies were done, I still had to clean the kitchen. I looked at my watch— it was five fifteen. By the time the kitchen was clean it was almost six,

and I hadn't even thought about starting dinner.

I guess it's a good thing everyone in
my family likes Cheerios, huh?

chapter six ᘓ

"Let me explain to you how mayonnaise works. Have you ever heard of a colloid?"

Aretha's dad, Mr. Timmons, stood at the kitchen counter with a food processor in front of him. Aretha, Ben, and I were sitting on tall kitchen stools on the other side of the counter. We were taking notes in our notebooks, and Ben was filming. "I don't want to miss any important information," he'd explained when he showed up at Aretha's with his camera. "Plus, who knows? Maybe we could end up doing our own cooking show. 'Aretha's Dad Teaches Kids to Cook,' or something like that."

"I don't know about a colloid," Ben said now. "But I've heard of a collard. Is that the same thing?"

Mr. Timmons laughed. "Not quite. You make a colloid when you dissolve one thing into another thing. When we're talking about liquids, it's more accurately called an emulsion."

Aretha and I both wrote like crazy in our notebooks. Ben popped off his chair so he could move in for a close-up.

Holding up an egg and a bottle of olive oil, Mr. Timmons said, "The interesting thing about mayonnaise is, here you have two things that don't typically mix. You've got your oil, and in this egg you have water. But because we're going to *slowly* dissolve the oil into the eggs, we're going to bring these two opposites together."

Then he broke three eggs into the food processor and punched the on button. Once the eggs were all mixed up, he started dripping olive oil into the feed tube on top.

"You have to be patient," Mr. Timmons told us. "Just a little bit of oil at a time."

It seemed like it took forever, but all of a sudden the stuff in the food processor turned all creamy and white.

"Cool!" Ben exclaimed, recording the mayo from all angles. "There's only one problem."

"What's that?" Mr. Timmons asked.

"Mayonnaise sort of makes me feel sick."

Mr. Timmons nodded. "Me too, but I know you guys are interested in science, and this is the most food science I know. So who wants to learn how to make hamburgers for lunch?"

We'd already made scrambled eggs, hard-boiled eggs, omelets, and egg salad (which was when Mr. Timmons decided he should to teach us how to make mayonnaise). To be honest, I was getting a little tired of eggs. Hamburgers sounded great.

After Mr. Timmons gave us all his best hamburger cooking tips (don't overhandle the meat, fry the burgers in butter, don't turn up the heat too high), and we had four burgers frying in a pan, Aretha said she thought we should have salad with our burgers in order to keep our meal nutritionally balanced. "One thing I'm supposed to do for my badge is make a meal healthier," she told us. "Adding a salad in this situation will definitely do the trick."

Mr. Timmons gave Aretha the thumbs-up. "Salad dressing is the easiest thing in the world," he said, handing me the olive oil and a bottle of balsamic vinegar. "Two parts oil to one part vinegar, and you've got salad dressing. All you've got to do is put it in a jar, put the lid on, shake the jar up, and there you have it—your very own colloid!"

"But since it's liquid, we call it an emulsion," Aretha said, writing in her notebook. "Right?"

"You got it, my little genius," Mr. Timmons said. "Now who wants to peel some carrots?"

After we finished eating lunch, me, Ben, and Aretha cleaned up the kitchen and tried to brainstorm egg recipes, but it turned out everybody was sick of eggs.

"How about an omelet with bacon and raspberries?" Ben asked as we were getting ready to leave. "Or a BLT omelet?"

"I don't think you can cook lettuce," Aretha told him. "It gets all slimy."

"You could use spinach instead of lettuce," I suggested. "People eat slimy spinach all the time. I mean, you know, the cooked stuff."

Of course, at our house, you'll find most of the slimy spinach in a bag at the bottom of the vegetable bin in the fridge.

That, you want to avoid.

When I got home, I decided to study my lab notes from my week of kitchen duty. Since I'd started cooking dinner, I'd learned a lot of stuff. First, there were all the lessons I learned about making spaghetti the first night. The next day, when I made the brownies for Evan, I learned about the importance of cleaning up as you go, or else you won't actually have time to make dinner. Last night, when I'd finally gotten around to trying homemade waffles, I learned that a tablespoon is not a spoon you'll find on a table, but an actual measuring spoon that's with all the other measuring spoons in the kitchen drawer.

Which might explain why my waffles came out sort of flat.

"Kind of like tortillas," Lyle had observed when I served them up. "Except with syrup."

It was my mom who figured out I'd used a cereal spoon to measure out the baking powder. "That would give you about a teaspoon of baking powder," she explained. "And the recipe called for a tablespoon, so three times as much. Baking powder is a leavening agent. Do you know what that means?"

"Leavening agent?" I asked. My mom raised her eyebrows—the universal signal in our house for "look it up."

So I looked it up. A leavening agent is what makes stuff puff up by producing carbon dioxide. I already knew about yeast, but it turns out that baking powder and baking soda are leavening agents too. Without them, cookies, waffles, bread, and cake would all fall flat.

Lesson learned.

Reading my lab notes, I felt like I'd had a pretty good week, even if I hadn't made anything explode yet. I knew deep down that exploded food probably wouldn't taste all that good, but I bet it was the funnest food to cook.

So if my week had been so scientifically successful, why did I have a bad feeling in the pit of my stomach?

Two words: Evan Forbes.

I'd made two batches of brownies already for Evan, and next week he wanted me to make him three. "I'm selling some of them to my buddies," he explained. "Fifty cents a pop. I'm raking in the dough, Mac."

To be honest, that didn't seem very fair to me. I was doing all the work. Why should Evan be making all the money?

Unfortunately, I didn't have the guts to ask him.

One thing I knew for sure was that Sarah was going to start getting suspicious if I made brownies nearly every afternoon. And if Sarah got suspicious, she'd start nosing around and figure out that Evan Forbes was a brownies bully. Then she'd tell my mom, and my mom would call Principal Patino, and Principal Patino would call Evan into the office, and then after school Evan would clobber me.

I needed a plan.

Fortunately, I was a scientific genius, so it only took me eight hours to come up with one. I was brushing my teeth, and I was thinking about what I was going to do the next day. Ben wanted me to go over to his apartment so we could work on our prizewinning recipe. He still didn't know what he wanted to make, and we needed to decide fast.

I thought about what Aretha said. Make something you like, but make it a little bit different. Give it a new twist.

Well, I liked brownies, or at least I used to like brownies before Evan Forbes started forcing me to bake them.

So why not work on a fantastizoid brownie recipe? That would give me just the excuse I needed for making a ton of

brownies. I could make fifty brownies a day and start stockpiling them in the freezer. By the end of the week, I might have enough brownies to give Evan for the rest of the year.

I'm a genius, I thought, spitting toothpaste into the sink. I bet there were a million ways to make brownies. Brownies with chocolate chips, brownies with marshmallows, brownies with broken-up peppermint candies.

And, okay, sure. Why not? We could even try brownies with bacon.

chapter seven

"Brownies are kind of boring, don't you think?" Ben was sitting on the couch in his apartment, drawing a new Derek the Destroyer comic book and watching Saturday morning cartoons. Derek the Destroyer is this superhero Ben made up a couple of years ago. In spite of his name, he's actually a good guy, and he's always saving the world from total annihilation. In the most recent series of Derek the Destroyer comics, Earth is under attack by an army of giant mold monsters who slime everything in their path as they fight for world domination.

It's totally cool.

"Boring? Brownies?" I shook my head like I couldn't believe how dumb Ben was being. "They're like the most exciting dessert product ever. They're practically a dessert *event.* Thick, rich, moist, chocolaty. Plus, they're easy to make, and I bet we could come up with an original recipe that will blow the judges' socks off."

Ben thought about this for a minute. "I wonder if we could come up with a brownie recipe that you could set on fire. Like, there's this dessert called cherries jubilee, and right before you serve it, you make it burst into flames."

"How do you do that?"

Ben shook his head. "I'm not sure. I guess you pour something on it that flames up and then burns out."

"And isn't poisonous," I added.

"Right. We can find out. Brownies jubilee. That has a nice ring to it, don't you think?"

I actually thought flaming brownies sounded like a great idea, but I was pretty sure that wasn't the direction I wanted to go in. Evan Forbes would definitely clobber me if I gave him burned-up brownies. "Maybe we should start with some simpler recipes and build up to brownies jubilee," I said. "Perfect our recipe and then add special effects to it."

"That's probably a good idea," Ben agreed. "I'll just go call Mrs. Klausenheimer, and we can get started."

"Why do you have to call Mrs. Klausenheimer?"

"In case you haven't noticed, my mom's at work, which means we are currently semi-unsupervised. My mom said if we even thought about turning on the oven, we had to call Mrs. Klausenheimer to come over and be the official adult."

Ben lives in an apartment building. His mom is the apartment building manager. Most of their neighbors are old people, and a couple of months ago when we did the dog slobber experiment, we went around to different apartments to get slobber samples. Mrs. Klausenheimer's dog was one of the scariest ones we met, a huge German shepherd with teeth the size of baseball bats.

Very sharp baseball bats.

"She's not going to bring Killer with her, is she?"

Ben looked worried. "I don't think so. Chocolate is really bad for dogs. She probably doesn't want to take the chance that he'll eat a bunch of brownies and have to go to the vet."

Five minutes later there was a knock on the door. "Bennie! I'm here!"

When Ben opened the door, Mrs. Klausenheimer shuffled in clutching an overstuffed purse and headed directly for the couch. "Now, you're making brownies, is that right? I know the most divine recipe. It calls for eggnog, whipped cream, and crème de menthe. Does your mother keep those things in her pantry, Bennie?"

"I don't think so, Mrs. Klausenheimer," Ben told her. "She mostly keeps normal stuff."

"Too bad, too bad." Mrs. Klausenheimer pulled a copy of *Celebrity Homes and Recreation Vehicles* magazine out of her purse. "Well, you boys run along and make your brownies. Don't get your fingers caught in the mixer!"

"She's our official adult?" I whispered as I followed Ben to the kitchen. "She's like the opposite of Sarah Fortemeyer. You could get away with anything!"

"I know, cool, right?" Ben asked with a grin. "Sometimes she babysits me, and we order six pizzas with all different kinds of toppings. Then we have a contest to see who can eat the most slices. After that, Mrs. Klausenheimer falls asleep and I can do whatever I want."

Sometimes I think Ben's the luckiest kid in the world.

All the ingredients for basic brownies were lined up on the kitchen counter. I grabbed my backpack, which I'd thrown on the kitchen table earlier. "So I figure we have time to try three

different kinds," I told Ben, dumping the contents of my backpack out on the table. "First, M&M's brownies. Second, marshmallow brownies. And third—"

"I got it!" exclaimed Ben. "Pizza brownies. Genius-zoid! Why didn't I think of that earlier! Pepperoni, mozzarella, delicious!"

"Yeah, except for the part where you start throwing up. Pizza brownies? Are you serious?"

"Perfectly serious," Ben said with a perfectly serious expression on his face. "Everybody loves pizza, everybody loves brownies. Why not combine the two?"

"I mentioned the part about throwing up, right?"

Ben shrugged. "I think you underestimate people, Mac. It's the twenty-first century. We eat all kinds of stuff now!"

I could see that Ben was not going

to be budged unless I figured a way to work around him. "Okay, how about this? We call the M&M's pepperoni, the marshmallows mozzarella, and for the tomato sauce . . ."

"Actual tomato sauce! It's sweet, right? It'll work, Mac, I'm telling you!"

"No, it won't," I said. "You have to trust me on this. But maybe we could chop up some maraschino cherries?"

Ben sniffed a couple of times, like the idea sort of offended him, but then he gave in. "Yeah, I think we have some maraschino cherries in the fridge," he admitted.

"Okay, we'll do pizza

brownies first," I told him. "And then we'll try a couple of other kinds."

"Do you think we're going to start getting sick of brownies?" Ben asked.

I was already sick of brownies, but I couldn't admit that without explaining the Evan Forbes situation. So I kept my mouth shut.

By the end of the afternoon, we had seventy-two brownies. The pizza brownies were okay, but Ben thought the next time we tried them, we ought to use marshmallow cream instead of marshmallows, spread it over the top of the baked brownies, and then put the M&M's and maraschino cherries on top.

My favorite brownies were the ones that just had marshmallows in them. Simple, gooey, delicious, and nothing at all like pizza.

"They're all fantastic, boys," Mrs. Kleisenheimer said when she woke up from her nap and sampled one of each. "Next time with the M&M brownies, add some more M&M's. You can never have too many M&M's, in my humble opinion."

"The question is, which ones will the judges like best?" Ben scratched his chin. "How does a recipe judge think? I like the pizza brownies a lot, but they need one more element. Something else that will really make them stand out."

"We could make them explode," I suggested.

Ben jumped about five feet in the air. "Exploding Pizza Brownies! Fantastizoid! Incredibaloo! Yes, Mac! Yes!"

I'm pretty sure he liked the idea.

I liked it too. I liked it especially when

I thought about a brownie exploding right as Evan Forbes was about to take a bite.

Ben thumped me on my back. "You're a genius, Mac. I've always said it."

"But I don't actually know how to make exploding brownies," I told him. "That could be a problem."

"How hard could it be?" Ben said with a shrug. "You mix in a little of this, a little of that, and whammo! Exploding brownie! Easy peasy."

"Maybe if we added bacon to the brownie mix, we could have sizzling brownies," I said. "Sizzling is almost as good as exploding."

"Sizzling and exploding are two entirely different things," Ben argued. "Still, you might have a point. A little bacon in our brownies could really make the flavor pop."

Okay, so maybe our brownies wouldn't explode, but they could definitely pop. Popping was a step in the right direction.

I just hoped Evan Forbes liked bacon.

chapter eighteen

The routine goes like this. I get off the school bus in the morning with a brown paper bag full of brownies. Instead of going directly into school, I look around to make sure no one is paying attention, and then I take a sharp right, then a sharp left, and walk twenty feet down an alley to the Dumpsters behind the cafeteria. Then I wait for Evan Forbes to show up.

The Dumpsters are the stinkiest part

of the school. I don't mind stinky stuff as much as other people do, because bad smells are a sign that some science is happening. In fact, spending so much time around the Dumpsters got me thinking. So why does stuff stink in the first place?

Here is what my research has turned up:

1. Stuff that stinks is usually stuff you shouldn't eat. So stinkiness may be nature's way of telling you to stay away so you won't eat something and immediately croak.

2. Some stinky things are actually okay to eat, like Limburger cheese, which stinks because of the bacteria that's used to make it. It's called *Brevibacterium linens,* which is the same bacteria that

makes people stink if they haven't taken a shower in a while.

3. Just because it's okay to eat Limburger cheese doesn't mean I'm going to.

4. I mean, have you ever smelled that stuff?

5. A lot of stinky stuff is in the process of decomposing. Tissues are breaking down and bacteria are eating everything they can get their hands on, which produces the gas that makes us plug our noses.

6. Bacteria are responsible for a lot of the world's stinkiness.

So maybe I'm being bullied into making brownies every day, but at least I'm getting to learn some interesting new science facts.

On Monday I stood by the Dumpsters, holding a bag with a dozen marshmallow brownies. I hoped Evan liked marshmallows. When I heard someone walking down the alley toward the Dumpsters, I automatically started worrying that Evan Forbes hated marshmallows, and my stomach started hurting like crazy because I thought this might be the day that he finally clobbered me.

It was only a matter of time.

"Mac?"

The voice was familiar, but it wasn't Evan's.

Mr. Reid came around the corner of the Dumpsters. "What are you doing back here, Mac? This area is off-limits to students."

"I was—uh—I was—just waiting."

"Waiting for what?"

"For a friend of mine." I held out the

bag. "I wanted to give him some of the brownies I made this weekend. Me and Ben are working on a recipe for this contest. If we win, we're going to each get five thousand dollars. I was thinking I might use my five thousand dollars to buy a chemistry set. Do you know anything about chemistry sets, Mr. Reid? Because I sure could use some advice—"

Mr. Reid cut me off. "Whoa there, Mac! Your mouth is going a hundred miles an hour, and I still can't figure out what you're doing here. Why would you meet a friend behind the Dumpsters to give him brownies?"

I couldn't think of an answer.

"Well?" Mr. Reid said.

"I like how it smells back here?" I said.

Which, you have to admit, was not a total lie.

Mr. Reid gave me a concerned, grandfatherly type look. "Mac, what's going on? I saw you out here once last week too. Is there something you want to tell me about?"

I wanted like anything to tell Mr. Reid about the Evan Forbes brownie situation. There was only one problem: I also wanted to live to be ten.

A lot of grown-ups will tell you that if you have a problem, you should tell an adult that you trust. Adults are there to help you. And I pretty much believe this, except in situations where someone will probably kill you if you tell.

I mean, what are the grown-ups going to do? Put Evan Forbes in jail? No, he's a kid, and all they'll do is talk to him and maybe make him stay after school for a week. And he'll make a big deal about how sorry he is, and how he'll never bully another kid again, and then guess what?

He'll clobber me.

Finally I came up with a big lie to tell Mr. Reid. "The thing is—and I kinda know this is against the rules—but I'm playing this spy game with some kids? And the brownies are like a cover? And this is one of our secret spy ring meet-up places?"

"You don't sound too sure of yourself, Mac," Mr. Reid said, looking doubtful.

"I guess I'm just worried I'm going to get in trouble."

Mr. Reid seemed to think about this. "I'll tell you what, Mac. I won't take you to Principal Patino's office this time, but I don't want to find you out here again. Is that understood?"

I nodded. "I promise."

"Then run on inside," Mr. Reid said,

smiling, like everything was okay now.

But everything was definitely not okay. First of all, as I walked back up the alley to the front of the school, Evan Forbes showed up.

"Hey! Where are you going with my brownies? I thought I told you to meet me at the Dumpsters. Well, hand 'em over, dude. And tomorrow, wait until I get here. Understood?"

"I can't," I told him. "Mr. Reid caught me standing there. He says he'll take me to the principal's office if he catches me again."

Evan grabbed the bag from me. "That's your problem, Big Mac. See ya tomorrow."

I slumped against the side of the building. I felt really, truly awful. I was lying to everybody, I was either going to get clobbered or sent to detention, and it was starting to look like I was going to have to give Evan Forbes brownies for the rest of my life.

I closed my eyes. "What am I going to do?" I asked out loud, like I hoped the wall would give me some advice.

When I opened my eyes, Aretha was standing in front of me. "I don't know, Mac. What are you going to do? I can tell you one thing—you need to do something, and fast."

I stared at her. "How much do you know?"

"Everything, I think." She glanced to her left, and then to her right, like a character in a spy movie. "I've been keeping an eye on you, Mac. It's never a good thing when Evan Forbes starts paying too much attention to a kid. I figured he was up to something, so I've been spying."

"I don't even know how I got into this mess," I told her. "Two weeks ago my life was completely normal."

We started walking to the front of the building. "Yeah, you definitely have a problem, Mac," Aretha said. "An Evan Forbes–size problem."

"So what do I do about it?"

"You meet me and Ben at the jungle gym at recess. With my great brain, your scientific know-how, and Ben's creativity, we'll figure something out."

And just like that, my stomach stopped hurting.

chapter nine

We found Ben dangling upside down from the top bar of the jungle gym.

"Jeez, Mac," he said when Aretha and I explained the situation. "Epic fail on the number one rule in the *The Big Book of Best Friend Rules*, buddy."

"Uh, the what?"

"*The Big Book of Best Friend Rules*. Keeping a secret is the number one no-no."

"I didn't know there was a *Big Book*

of Best Friend Rules," I said, climbing up to the top and taking a seat next to him.

Ben tapped his head. "I keep it all up here. Rule number one: no secrets. Rule number two: best friends stick together, even if it causes bodily harm."

Aretha pulled herself up so she was dangling from the bar across from me. "I bet if you stood up to Evan, he'd back off. My mom says that most bullies are all talk."

"And so what if he punches you?" Ben added. "He's not going to punch you every day for the rest of your life. I predict three days' worth of punches, tops. Then it's over and you go back to your regular life."

"This isn't making me feel better, guys." I leaned back and looked at the sky. To the west, I saw a bunch of

nimbostratus clouds, which meant it would probably rain later.

I thought it was sort of awesome that I knew that fact.

"I wish I could just do science all the time," I told Ben and Aretha. "I wish I didn't have stupid problems that I don't know how to solve."

"I know! Maybe you should think of Evan Forbes as a scientific challenge!" Aretha said, her voice all of a sudden excited. "You formulate a question, do your background research—"

"Construct a hypothesis," I continued, "test your hypothesis through experiments, and then analyze your data and draw a conclusion."

"And then eat a doughnut," Ben finished up. "Because what you guys are describing sounds like a lot of work. You're gonna need a doughnut when you're done. Probably one with frosting and sprinkles."

"What we're describing is the scientific method," Aretha informed him. She pulled herself up so she was sitting on top of the jungle gym and turned to me. "So what's the question you're going to start with?"

I thought about it for a minute. "How about, 'What's the best way to stop a bully from bullying you?'"

Aretha nodded. "That's good. Now, how about research?"

"I could read some articles on the Internet," I said. "And maybe ask Mrs. Patino and Mr. Reid. They've probably seen a lot of bullies over the years."

"You could ask other kids, too," Ben said. "Everybody's got at least one story about somebody being mean to them."

"Yeah! Remember how you were mean to Chester Oliphant at the beginning of the school year?" I asked Ben. That was back in the days when Ben was new to the school and acted like he didn't care if anyone liked him or not.

Ben's face turned red. "I don't want to think about that. It's sort of embarrassing."

"But it could be helpful to our research!" Aretha exclaimed. "Why *were* you so mean to Chester?"

"I don't know," Ben said with a shrug.

"I was just acting all stupid and stuff. I didn't know what else to do."

Later, during social studies, Ben passed me a note. When I unfolded it, I saw he had written in big letters at the top of the paper: FOR SCIENTIFIC RESEARCH ONLY. READ AND DESTROY!

Then there was this list that was titled "Why I Was Stupid and Sort of Mean When I First Moved Here."

1. I was scared other people would be mean to me first.
2. Everyone was sort of ignoring me.
3. Chester Oliphant is the only kid in our class shorter than I am.
4. I missed my dad.

Ben's list gave me an amazing idea. I could put together a questionnaire and give it to all the kids in my class. It could be questions for kids who had been bullied and questions for kids who'd been bullies. Most of the kids in my class were pretty nice, but looking around, I saw one or two who were friendly now, but had been sort of mean in second or third grade. Also, there were girls like

Stacey Windham, who could be super nice to her friends one day and then totally ignore them the next day. Why couldn't she be nice every day?

All of a sudden I felt better than I had in forever. That's the great thing about science, in my opinion. When you take the scientific approach, instead of sitting around all day feeling rotten about a problem, you look it straight in the eye. You ask questions. You get to the bottom of things.

I was copying down the homework assignment, when a question popped into my mind. What would happen if I told Evan Forbes I wasn't going to bring him brownies anymore?

My hypothesis? I'd get clobbered.

But here's the weird thing: My next thought was, maybe I should do an experiment.

Maybe I should tell Evan Forbes no.

My stomach started hurting just by thinking that. But it didn't hurt as bad as it usually did when I thought about Evan. The thing about me and Evan Forbes was, we were like a colloid. We were two things that didn't really mix together unless you forced them to. We were mayonnaise. We were whipped cream (which, in case you're wondering, is a gas dissolved into a liquid). We were gelatin (solid dissolved into a liquid, FYI).

Now, some things when you force them together turn out okay.

And some things, like me and Evan, are a disaster.

Scientifically speaking, I was pretty sure it was time for us to go our separate ways.

Okay, then. When I got home, I'd do the following:

1. Come up with a list of questions about bullying to hand out to all the kids in my class.
2. Brainstorm all the horrible things that could happen to me if I stopped giving Evan Forbes brownies.
3. Come up with a deadline for no longer giving Evan Forbes brownies.
4. Try not to think too much about getting clobbered when I stop giving Evan Forbes brownies.
5. Make dinner.

I thought about the stuff I could make for dinner. I could make hamburgers and salad, or waffles or spaghetti. I could try a new recipe, liked baked chicken and mashed potatoes.

I leaned back in my chair, starting

to get hungry as I pictured all the good things we could eat that night.

And that's when I got my craziest idea ever.

I could invite Evan Forbes over to eat. I could do my scientific research in the comfort of my very own home.

That's too crazy, I thought. Besides, what would be the point? So Evan Forbes could bully me in front of my family? So he could find things to make fun of, like Margaret's potty training chair that Sarah kept parked in front of the TV?

And then this funny picture came into my head. Remember that day Evan got held back at lunchtime because he hadn't turned in his homework? I'd sort of forgotten about it, but all of a sudden I remembered how his face looked when I turned around, like he was about to cry.

Maybe Evan Forbes wasn't so tough after all.

I'd invite him over and see if I could find out.

chapter ten

Evan Forbes sounded confused when I called him that afternoon.

"You want me to do what?"

"Come over to my house for dinner," I said, my voice sounding sort of squeaky. "I'll be cooking. I mean, you seem to like my cooking a lot, right?"

"Yeah, I guess—I mean, no! I mean, you're such a dweeb, MacGuire! People don't go over to other people's houses for dinner!"

"You mean your family never goes to anybody else's house to eat?"

"My parents work late every night. My nanny makes me dinner."

Evan Forbes had a nanny?

"You have a nanny?"

"Well, she used to be my nanny. Now that I'm older, I guess she's my—I don't know. Whatever you call someone who takes care of you and drives you around and stuff."

"Your assistant?" I thought Evan might like the sound of that.

He did.

"Yeah, my assistant! That's it. She's kind of like my assistant and my personal chef. She cooks dinner every night. So why would I eat dinner someplace else?"

I had to think about that for a minute. "Because it's interesting to try new food and to see how other people live?"

Evan snorted. "You think I want to see how a dweeb like you lives, MacGuire? You're totally gonzo."

"I'm a pretty good cook," I halfway lied. I was pretty much a brownie expert by now, but other stuff? Not so much. "What kind of stuff does your assistant make for dinner?"

"I don't know," Evan said. It sounded like he was stalling. "You know, frozen stuff that you microwave. Pita pockets. Chicken nuggets." He paused. "What are you making for dinner tonight?"

"I was thinking about some baked chicken and mashed potatoes."

"And biscuits?"

I could practically hear Evan sniffing the air, like the smell of biscuits was coming through the phone.

"Yeah, sure," I told him. "I could try some biscuits."

"Okay, whatever," Evan said. "I'll be there at six. But it better be good, MacGuire!"

As soon as I hung up the phone, I yelled for Sarah. "I need help!"

Sarah rushed into the kitchen. "What's wrong? Did you hurt yourself?"

"Worse! I need to make biscuits, and I don't know how!"

Sarah grinned. "Have no fear! My hundred-year-old granny was a champion biscuit maker. I know all the tricks."

"Really?" I couldn't believe my good luck.

"No, not really. My grandmother's sixty-four and never cooked a day in her life. But my dad makes biscuits for breakfast on Sundays. It's easy peasy."

After that, Sarah started bossing me around. Get the flour! We need baking soda and baking powder! Don't forget the salt!

"And we'll need to make buttermilk," she told me. "So get out the milk and the lemon juice from the fridge."

"How about the butter?" I asked.

"There's no butter in buttermilk," Sarah said. "Buttermilk is the sour milk left over after butter's been churned."

"We're putting sour milk in the biscuits?"

Sarah nodded. "It'll give your biscuits a little zing, Mac. Trust me."

I have never trusted Sarah Fortemeyer a day in my life.

"The thing about buttermilk is that it's not something you usually keep around," Sarah said. "So it's easier just to make a buttermilk substitute by putting a little

lemon juice in your milk to curdle it."

"This is not sounding delicious," I told her.

"What did I say, Mac? You've got to trust me on this. I know what I'm talking about."

We added one tablespoon of lemon juice to a cup and a half of milk and let it sit for five minutes. The weird thing was, when we looked at the milk after five minutes, it was kind of clumpy.

"That's because it's curdled," Sarah explained. "The lemon juice separates the milk into curds."

"What does that mean exactly?" I asked, but Sarah shrugged, like she didn't know.

So of course I had to look it up.

Remember how, on Saturday, we learned about colloids and emulsions? What I learned today was, curdling is like the opposite thing. When something is curdled, the emulsion or the colloid gets separated again. In this case, it's the lemon juice that's breaking stuff up.

If only I could figure out how to curdle me and Evan Forbes.

It didn't take very long to make the biscuits. Sarah let me use the food processor to mix up the butter, flour, baking soda, baking powder, and salt.

"The trick to good biscuits is to not overhandle your dough," she explained. "I'm sure there's a scientific reason for that, but I don't know what it is. What I know is, if you use a food processor to mix up your dry ingredients with your butter, it's faster than doing it by hand, and your biscuits turn out softer."

After we were done mixing the butter and flour, we dumped it in a bowl, and then dumped the buttermilk into the flour. The buttermilk was all lumpy and bumpy, and I was doing some serious trusting that Sarah knew what she was talking about, because right now I was thinking these biscuits might taste pretty gross.

Sarah showed me how to roll out the dough and use a glass to cut out the biscuits. We baked them for eight minutes and then brushed them with melted butter when they were done.

Here is what I learned: Freshly baked biscuits smell better than anything in the world. They are the opposite of stinky. They are in an entirely different universe from stinky.

I couldn't believe I was going to be wasting them on Evan Forbes.

Neither could my mom.

"You invited someone to dinner?" she practically screeched when I told her that Evan would be here at six. She'd just walked in the door, and I thought I'd better break the news to her right away. "Mac, I'm exhausted! And the house is a mess. And who is this Evan Forbes, anyway? I've never heard of him."

"He's this kid from school," I explained. "And he thinks it's kind of—uh—neat that I'm learning how to cook."

"I've got an idea," my mom said, setting down her briefcase and looking through the day's mail. "He can come over on Saturday. We could make home-made pizza. I've been wanting to try that, and it could be a lot of fun to do it with some friends."

"I think he's really looking forward to biscuits."

My mom looked at me. "You made biscuits?" She sniffed the air. "You made biscuits!"

It was like she morphed into an entirely new person.

It turned out that freshly baked homemade biscuits held powers far beyond those of mortal men.

My mom took a deep breath. "Okay, Mac, Evan can come over. It sounds like you've done a lot of work to make a nice dinner."

"And he doesn't get a home-cooked meal very often," I said. I thought it couldn't hurt to soften my mom up a little more. "His parents aren't ever home for dinner the way you and Lyle are. His nanny just heats him up chicken nuggets."

"Oh, that poor

child," my mom said. She came over to me and gave me a hug. "You're very sweet for inviting him to eat with us."

I shrugged. "I like to be a good friend when I can."

What I liked was not getting clobbered. Maybe if Evan Forbes liked my biscuits, he wouldn't feel like clobbering me so much.

Or maybe he'd make me start bringing him biscuits every day instead of brownies.

My stomach started hurting again. Do you know why your stomach hurts? Sometimes it's from excess gas because you ate something like beans that have a lot of fiber and take longer to digest.

And sometimes it's because your stomach fills up with acid that your body has produced because your brain has told it to be afraid.

To be really honest, I was tired of being afraid.

Anyway, it was time to make the mashed potatoes.

Mashed potatoes are super easy to make, by the way. You peel four or five potatoes and chop them into chunks. Then you boil the chunks for about fifteen minutes, until they're nice and soft. All that's left to do after that is pour in about half a cup of milk, and some butter and salt, and get mashing. I wanted to use the electric mixer, but my mom thought it would be safer to use the hand masher.

I didn't mind. It took my mind off the Evan Forbes problem.

Actually, it kind of gave me an Evan Forbes solution. Mashing potatoes takes a while, and while I was mashing, I started thinking about other stuff, like what questions I was going to ask on my bullying research questionnaire.

That's when I had a genius thought—I was going to have my very own, live bully right there in my house.

I could get Evan to help me come up with questions. I mean, who would know better what questions to ask about bullying than a genuine bully?

Genius!

Or crazy.

I was pretty sure it was one or the other.

chapter eleven

Evan Forbes ate eleven biscuits.

Eleven.

He smeared the first two with butter, and the next nine he just sort of inhaled straight from the basket.

It was actually pretty impressive.

"So, Evan, Mac tells us you boys are in the same class?" my mom asked in her polite hostess voice. She was buttering up her third biscuit.

Not that I was counting.

Evan shook his head. "Not the same class—just the same grade," he told her through a mouthful of crumbs. "I'm in Mr. Burch's class. He's a lot cooler than Mrs. Tuttle. She's got this weird thing about frogs."

"She's okay," I said. Actually, I think Mrs. Tuttle is awesome, but I thought it would be rude to argue with my guest.

Also, I didn't want to get clobbered.

It took Evan only about three minutes to eat. After he ate eleven biscuits, he chowed down the chicken in three bites and slurped up three servings of mashed potatoes in under sixty seconds.

He spent the rest of dinner making silly faces at Margaret to make her laugh.

And when dinner was over, he helped clear the table.

It was almost like he was an actual human being.

"You got an Xbox, Mac?" he asked when we were done taking the plates to the sink. "That's how I like to wind down after dinner—playing a few hours of video games."

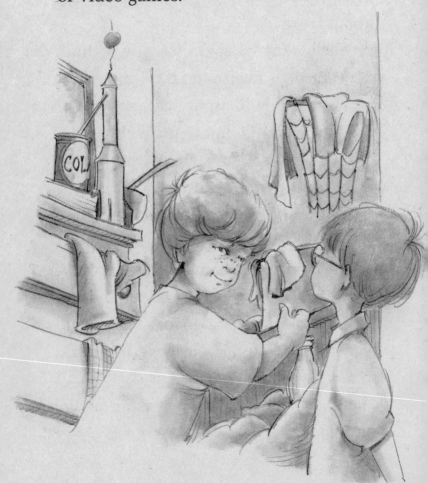

"What about homework?" I asked.

Evan shrugged. "What about it? Some people do it, I don't. Next subject."

"We don't actually have an Xbox," I told him. "Or any gaming systems. My mom is sort of against them."

I waited for Evan to explode. Amazingly, he just shrugged again and said, "So what do you want to do? My nanny—er, assistant—isn't picking me up until seven thirty."

Here's the funny thing: Evan Forbes looked smaller in my house than he did at school. Maybe that's why I actually had the guts to ask him to help me with my survey.

"Let me get this straight," he said as he followed me up the stairs to my room. "You want me to help you come up with questions about bullies?"

"Not just about bullies," I told him.

"But about kids who've been bullied."

He seemed to think about this for a second. "Yeah, I could help you. I mean, I got bullied a lot in second grade. Remember Jason Thedrow?"

"Sort of. But he doesn't go to our school anymore, does he?"

"Nah, he moved. But he was, like, totally all over my case in first and second grade."

I had to use all my willpower not to turn around and stare at him. Evan Forbes used to get bullied?

Totally weird.

I opened the door to my room and waved Evan in. A person's reaction to my room is a big test for whether or not we can be friends. If you are the sort of person who likes rooms that are neat and tidy, with all the clothes put away and all the books in the bookshelves, we're probably not going to get along all that well. Because my room is the total opposite of that.

In other words, if you can deal with chaos, we'll get along just fine.

"Awesome!" Evan exclaimed as he looked around. "I wish I could have my room like this."

That's when I had a very strange thought. Question: Was it possible that Evan Forbes and I might become friends?

"I mean, like, I never knew that a dweeb like you could have such a cool bedroom."

Answer: highly doubtful.

Evan walked around, admiring my mold museum, which is two shelves of mold samples I've been growing for a few months now, and checking out my collection of the Mysteries of Planet Zindar books.

"I have to keep my room totally neat," he told me. "Like, not one thing out of place. My dad does an inspection every night when he gets home from work, whether I'm still awake or not."

"What happens if your room doesn't pass inspection?"

"Then I have to clean it up immediately. Even if it's eleven at night and I'm asleep. My dad makes me wake up and make everything perfect."

I thought about my mom and dad and Lyle. None of them could care less whether or not my room is clean. Mostly all they care about is whether or not I'm happy and if I'm doing good at school.

All of a sudden I felt totally lucky.

"So, anyway, you want to work on that survey?" I asked as Evan dive-bombed onto my bed. "I kind of need to get it done."

Evan sat up and shrugged. "Not really, but I guess I owe you for the biscuits, so, like, whatever."

I thought he owed me for a whole lot more than the biscuits, but I decided not to mention it.

We spent the next twenty minutes coming up with questions. We had two lists, questions for kids who had been bullied and questions for kids who had bullied other kids.

"Maybe we ought to have questions for kids who've had both things happen," I suggested. "Like, maybe one year you might have been really mean to somebody, and the next year somebody was really mean to you."

"I hope somebody's jumping all over Jason Thedrow at his new school," Evan said, nodding. "He totally deserves it."

I stared at him.

He totally didn't get it.

Here's the funny thing: All of a sudden I realized that my stomach didn't hurt. It hadn't hurt all night, even though Evan had been in my personal space the whole time.

I had to wonder, scientifically speaking, what was going on.

Scientifically speaking, I'm pretty sure what was happening was pretty simple.

I wasn't scared of Evan Forbes anymore.

There were a lot of good explanations for this. One, the odds that Evan Forbes was going to clobber me in my own home were pretty small. Two, the odds that Evan Forbes was going to clobber me in my own home after eating eleven biscuits I'd made myself were even smaller.

So, we're talking minimal fear factor here.

But there was another thing. Eating dinner with Evan, showing him my room, learning a little bit about his family—well, he was actually seeming sort of human to me. Like a real person.

And sure, you can be afraid of a real person, but it's hard to be afraid of a real person who spent half of dinner stuffing his face with biscuits and the other half making funny faces at your little sister.

Thinking about how Evan made Margaret laugh, I came to a decision. Tomorrow, no brownies. No waiting by the Dumpsters, no stomachache, no nothing.

Tomorrow I'd pretend me and Evan Forbes were friends.

I mean, at least we weren't enemies anymore, right? And scientifically speaking, there's one thing I know for sure about friends, and that's that friends don't clobber each other.

At least that's what I was counting on. I'd have to look it up in *The Big Book of Best Friend Rules.*

chapter twelve

So that thing about me pretending to be Evan Forbes's friend so he wouldn't clobber me? Turns out I didn't have to pretend. He was waiting for me when I got off the bus at school this morning.

"Yo, Mac! Buddy!" he called when he saw me. "I had this great idea last night when I got home from your place. You and me can start a baking business! Brownies and biscuits, dude. We'll make a killing! And I'll help bake. I'll meet you at your house this afternoon, and we can get started."

"Well, uh, I'm sort of supposed to go over to Ben's house this afternoon," I told him as we walked into the building together. Evan held the front door open for me, which was totally weird. "We're doing this recipe contest, and we need to finalize our plans."

"Sounds great," Evan said. "What time should I be there?"

So that problem where Evan Forbes was my enemy? It was possible that my problem now was that he was my friend.

"Evan Forbes is coming over to my apartment this afternoon?" Ben asked when I told him at lunch. "Since when did Evan Forbes start hanging around with people like you and me?"

I told him about asking Evan to come

to dinner the night before. Aretha, who was sitting at her usual spot one table over, leaned toward us and said, "Brilliant plan, Mac! You ought to get the Nobel Peace Prize for that one."

"Yeah, but now he wants to go into business with me."

Aretha thought about this for a minute. "Just tell him you're a scientist and you don't have time to start a business."

"Yeah," Ben said. "Tell him you could help him get started, though. I'll do the PR."

I stared at him. "PR?"

"Yeah, you know—public relations. Publicity, advertising." Ben chomped on a pretzel stick. "If this recipe contest thing doesn't pan out, I might need a new line of work."

"So how is the recipe contest coming along?" Aretha asked.

"Oh, man! I can't believe I haven't told you guys this!" Ben's face lit up. "I've got the best recipe idea ever: salted pizza brownies with bacon."

I stared at Ben over my tuna fish sandwich. "Salted brownies?"

Ben nodded. "I've been reading all this stuff about food trends online? And salt is big. I mean, it's huge, and when it comes to chocolate, it's humongous."

"But won't the bacon add salt to the brownies?" I asked. Not that I was committed to the idea of putting bacon into a perfectly good pizza brownies recipe. But I like to be logical.

"The more salt the better, that's my motto!" Ben exclaimed. "The thing is, last night I tried out the pizza brownie recipe the way we talked about—I used marshmallow fluff on top, which worked great, and sprinkled it with extra M&M's just like Mrs. Klausenheimer said. And it was good, but it lacked a special something. So I made another batch, but this time I added an extra teaspoon of salt and half a cup of crumbled bacon. What can I say, Mac? They were genius brownies."

"Too much salt's bad for your heart."

Evan Forbes sat down in the seat next to me and opened up his lunchbox. "It's bad because it elevates your blood pressure. At least that's what my nanny—er, my assistant—says."

"But a little extra salt every once in a while is okay," Ben argued. At the same time he was looking at me like, *Really? Now we have to have lunch with him?* "You

only eat one brownie at a time, right?"

"Not if you're me," Evan told him, taking a huge bite of a turkey sub. "I eat 'em by the dozens. But hey, me and Mac will give your brownies a try this afternoon, and if we like 'em, then we can definitely move forward with the recipe."

You know that cartoon thing where steam comes out of somebody's ears?

That's how you should imagine Ben looking right at that very second.

I glanced over at Aretha. You could tell she was finding this all very interesting. "You guys mind if I tag along this afternoon? I might be able to get something out of it for my food badge." She turned to Evan. "I'm a Girl Scout."

"That's cool," Evan said. "Sure, you can come."

Then he crushed his milk carton and threw it at Mason Cutwelder's head. Mason yelled when the carton hit him, and Evan called out, "Sorry, dude! I was aiming for the trash can."

Only the trash can was in the opposite direction.

"Okay, I gotta go play some ball," Evan said, standing up. "You wanna play, Mac?"

I shook my head. "I, uh, have some homework I need to do."

"That's cool. I'll meet you on the bus after school."

Me, Ben, and Aretha all watched Evan walk out of the cafeteria. Then Ben turned to me and said, "You have got a serious problem on your hands, Mac. I don't know what's worse— having him for an enemy or having him for a friend."

Instead of going out to the playground for recess, I went to the library with my notebook. I needed to do some serious thinking.

First, I made a list called Good Things Right Now. That list included stuff like:

1. I am no longer worried about Evan Forbes clobbering me.
2. I know how to make the following things for dinner: chicken and mashed potatoes,

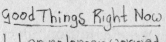

Good Things Right Now

1. I am no longer worried about Evan Forbes clobbering me.

Bad Things Right Now

1. Evan Forbes is my friend.
2. Evan Forbes wants to start a business with me.
3. Evan Forbes wants to take over my life.

spaghetti, waffles, biscuits, and Cheerios with milk.

3. I make the best brownies of any fourth-grade scientist in the United States, maybe the world.

4. I have about a hundred ideas for next year's science fair, including experiments with yeast, baking

powder, baking soda, lemon juice, colloids, and emulsions.

The Bad Things list looked like this:

1. Evan Forbes is my friend.
2. Evan Forbes wants to start a business with me.
3. Evan Forbes wants to take over my life.
4. I still haven't figured out how to make brownies explode.

The good things on my Good Things list were definitely really good.

But the bad things on my Bad Things list?

I was pretty sure the first three were going to ruin my life.

chapter thirteen

Riding the bus home this afternoon, I started reading through some of the bullying questionnaires that kids had filled out. I'd passed the questions around this morning, and by lunchtime twenty people had answered them and turned in their papers.

It turns out kids have a lot to say about kids being mean to other kids. To me, the most interesting facts were:

1. Everybody answered "yes" to the question, "Has another kid ever been mean to you (called you names, hit or pushed you, threatened you)?"
2. Twelve of the twenty responders answered "yes" to the question, "Have you ever been mean to another kid?"
3. When asked why they'd been mean to another kid, every single person answered, "I don't know."

I thought about the reasons Ben had given me for being mean to Chester Oliphant. The funny thing is, none of them really had anything to do with Chester. They all had to do with Ben. It wasn't like he had anything personal against Chester.

He just had something personal against himself.

I took a quick look at Evan, who was sitting next to me. He was busy poking the kid in the seat in front of us with a ballpoint pen. The kid was totally ignoring him, which just made Evan poke him harder.

I thought about how I never stood up for myself when Evan was being mean to me. Now I sort of wish I had, even if it meant getting clobbered.

"Quit it," I told Evan now. "That kid didn't do anything to you."

Evan looked at me. "The back of his head is bugging me."

"Well, it's bugging me that you keep poking him. Leave him alone."

"Okay," Evan said, shrugging. "Whatever."

Evan started tapping the bus window with his pen, and the kid who'd been getting poked turned around and gave me a quick smile.

Maybe instead of a Labrador whisperer, I should be a bully whisperer.

When Evan and I got to Ben's apartment, Aretha was already there. So was Mrs. Klausenheimer.

And so was Killer.

As soon as he saw Killer, Evan pulled me back out into the hallway. "You didn't say anything about dogs. I can't be in the same room as a dog."

"Are you allergic?"

"No, not exactly. It's just—well, me and dogs don't mix. I don't like them, and they don't like me."

In other words, Evan Forbes was scared.

"Listen," I told him. "Killer's actually a really nice dog. He looks like he'd tear your head off if he got a chance, but he's not like that at all."

"That dog? Nice? I don't think so!"

Now it's true that Killer is a humongous German shepherd with the biggest teeth you've ever seen. And it's true he looks like the sort of dog that would eat you for lunch. But inside all that fur and those razorlike incisors beats a canine heart of gold.

"You don't have to be afraid of Killer, I promise," I told Evan. "All it takes is a treat, and he'll be your friend for life."

"I'm not afraid." Evan's face was

totally red. "I just don't like dogs."

"If you're not afraid, then come back inside and I'll show you how nice Killer is. We can do a kind of experiment. That is, if you're really not afraid."

Evan didn't have a choice. He followed me back into Ben's apartment.

I went into the kitchen and got a couple of pieces of cooked bacon from Ben's bacon collection in the fridge. Ben liked to have at least half a pound of fried bacon ready at any time, in case he got any new bacon recipe inspirations. Tearing a piece in half, I called, "Come here, Killer!" Killer came galloping over to where I stood, practically knocking me over.

"Here's a treat, boy!" I told him, and held out a piece of bacon. He slurped it out of my hand, and when he was done gulping it down, he licked me all over my face.

Did I mention that Killer is a very slobbery dog?

Then I handed the other piece of bacon to Evan. "If you give this to Killer, he'll be your friend for life."

"Maybe I don't want a friend for life."

I gave Evan a hard look. "I thought you said you weren't afraid."

Evan sighed. "I'm not. Give me the stupid bacon."

His hand was shaking. "Here, Killer," he whispered in a squeaky voice.

Killer snatched the bacon from him, gulped it down, and then covered Evan Forbes with kisses. He knocked Evan down and licked him all over his face and hands.

At first Evan was doing this squeaky scream thing, and Mrs. Klausenheimer looked worried, like maybe we should pull Killer off him. But then all of a sudden Evan started laughing.

"You're slobbering on me, you stupid dog!"

And that was all it took.

Evan Forbes and Killer had bonded.

For the rest of the afternoon, while Ben,

Aretha, and I made brownies, Evan played with Killer in the living room while Mrs. Klausenheimer watched from the couch. When it was time to go home, she smiled at him and said, "If I had a grandson, I'd want him to be just like you, Evan. You're so good with Killer. If you were my grandson, you could come over every afternoon and play with him. I can't give him all the exercise he needs."

Evan was quiet for a minute. Then he said, "I could come over in the afternoons and play with Killer. I could sort of pretend I was your grandson. I never see my real grandparents, anyway."

Mrs. Klausenheimer bounced on the couch with excitement. "Oh, that would be lovely! I'll bake you cookies every day! Do you like oatmeal raisin?"

Riding the elevator down to the ground

floor, Evan said, "I guess I can't go into the baking business with you, Mac, now that me and Killer are going to be hanging out every day."

"That's okay," I told him. "I'm getting a little sick of brownies."

"Those pizza ones are pretty good, though," Evan said. "Except I don't think you should use real pepperoni."

"That was Ben's idea. He likes to experiment."

Evan nodded. "I can tell. Who knew a bacon milk shake would taste so good, though, right?"

"You learn something new every day," I agreed.

chapter fourteen

The phone rang while I was scrambling eggs. Scrambled eggs is now my go-to meal on days when I have lots of homework or have spent most of the afternoon hanging out with Ben or walking Lemon Drop.

Here's the trick to great scrambled eggs: Keep the heat low and cook 'em slow.

That's all there is to it.

"Mac, phone's for you," Sarah called

from the living room, where she and Margaret were having a fashion show. "It's a girl!"

The way she said, "It's a girl" was all singsongy and romantic.

I pretty much broke out in hives just from the sound of her voice.

"It's Aretha, so quit breaking out in hives," Aretha said when I grabbed the phone from Sarah. "I'm calling because I need help."

I turned the heat way down under the eggs. "All right, but I can't talk for long. I'm putting dinner on the table."

Okay, that sounded sort of weird.

"I need to figure out how to make exploding brownies," Aretha said. "Or some kind of crazy food. It's for the food science part of this badge I'm working on. I could do something boring like a presentation on lemon juice, but I want drama. I almost fell asleep at our last meeting, the presentations were so boring."

"So you want dramatic food?"

"That's right, Mac. I want food that will make everybody spin in their seats. Can you help me?"

"Meet me at the playground at recess tomorrow," I told her. "I'll have a report."

As I spooned the eggs onto the plates, I had a strange feeling. It was like I was remembering something I used to know but had sort of forgotten.

Like, oh yeah, I'm a scientist.

If I'd been wearing an apron, I would have flung it off. It wasn't that I was tired of cooking. I sort of liked cooking. But every night?

Not so much.

At dinner, I looked around the table and said, "I have an announcement.

From now on, I'll cook dinner two nights a week. If we have pizza and Cheerios all the other nights, that's fine with me. I am a scientist, and I have work to do. Cooking is a full-time job."

My mom thought about this. "It's true, cooking has been taking up a lot of your time. And your scientific work is important."

"Maybe I could make some freezer meals on the weekends," Lyle said. "There was an article in the paper the other day about a woman who does all her cooking for the month on one day—stews, casseroles, you name it. Then she puts everything in the freezer, and every morning she takes something out to thaw."

"You'd need a pretty big freezer to pull that off," I pointed out.

"Ours is big enough for a couple of

casseroles at least," Lyle said. "If your mom makes dinner Sunday nights, then we're set."

"Great," I said, pushing my chair away from the table. "Now I need to go make some food explode."

When you're a genius fourth-grade scientist, you keep files about all sorts of scientific matters. I keep my files in a shoe box in my closet, next to the shoe boxes filled with my dried worm collection and the shoe boxes with my dried fungus collection.

I have a very interesting closet. Though it does smell sort of funny.

I pulled out my scientific files shoe box and dumped its contents on my bed. There was stuff I'd clipped out of the newspaper and from magazines, like articles about Pluto losing its planet status (totally unfair, in my opinion), and notes

I'd taken when I was coming up with ideas for my mold museum (my favorite idea was having the museum in the bathroom, because mold likes humid places, but my mom said no way). There were ads for chemistry sets I wasn't going to be allowed to get until I was fifty, but I still liked to dream about.

And then there were my notebooks. I like to get those really little spiral notebooks that you can put in your back pocket. That way, if I get a scientific genius idea or come across some scientifically super-important information, I can write it down right away.

I started flipping through the articles and my notebooks to see if I could find anything about exploding food. I found something about exploding soda cans, and how to make an exploding cake using dry ice, which sounded way too awesome and too dangerous for any adult to give it the thumbs-up.

Okay, I said to myself, lying back against my pillow, what are we trying to accomplish here? Aretha wants drama and excitement, but the fact is, she's really trying to demonstrate something about food science. So what do I know about food science from personal experience?

I knew about emulsions and colloids. I knew how to curdle milk. I knew that if you didn't put enough baking powder in your waffle batter, your waffles would fall flat. But.

But!

What if you put in too much?

"So you're saying I should make exploding waffles?" Aretha asked me the next day at recess. We were sitting on the swings, with one empty swing between us so that no one would think we were swinging together.

I nodded, and Aretha smiled. "I like it," she said. "I like it a lot. It's about time someone did something to stir my troop up, and this ought to do the trick."

Just then Ben showed up. When Aretha told him about the exploding waffle idea, he got this big grin on his face. "I have a stupendazoid idea. You ought to add food coloring. Imagine it— exploding green waffles. I could film it and put it on YouTube. We'd be famous!"

"Green is the color of the Girl Scout uniform," Aretha said. "Plus, it might add a little more pizzazz to the whole project. Let's do it!"

At lunch, we went to the library to find a good waffle recipe on the Internet. As it turns out, there are over two mil-

lion waffle recipes on the Internet, so
we just checked out the first five and
picked the simplest one. Then we did
some research on baking powder so that
Aretha understood the science behind
the waffle explosion.

"So baking powder is made by

combining baking soda with an acid," Aretha said, taking notes as she talked. "When you add a liquid like water or milk, the acid and the base interact, and that creates carbon dioxide, which makes the stuff fizz up."

She looked up from her notes. "Basically, if our experiment works, the baking powder will produce a whole lot of carbon dioxide."

"Which is a kind of gas," Ben added.

"Which will make the waffles explode instead of just rise while they're baking," I finished up. "At least, that's our hypothesis."

Aretha grinned. "I'm glad we're doing this at Ben's house and not mine."

Ben was the only one of us with a waffle iron and a mom who wouldn't go nuts over somebody exploding waffles in her kitchen.

"So do you think we could explode brownies by putting in too much baking powder?" Ben asked as we walked back to Mrs. Tuttle's class. "Because our recipe's due pretty soon, and I'm not feeling all that confident about it."

"One, I don't think exploding brownies will taste all that good," I told him. "And two, the problem with your recipe is the pepperoni. Bacon is fine, but pepperoni is going too far."

Ben thought about this for a minute. "You could be right. Maybe I should take out the pepperoni and add some beef jerky."

"Have you ever thought about just making plain brownies?" Aretha asked. "Maybe with chocolate frosting to jazz them up a little bit?"

Ben and I looked at each other. Plain brownies with chocolate frosting?

"No way," Ben said.

"I don't think so," I said.

"No offense or anything," Ben told Aretha, "but really? I'm trying to win a recipe contest and that's what you come up with?"

Aretha shrugged. "Simple is good. Simple works."

"Simple's boring," I told her. "We need brownies that make a statement. We need life-altering brownies, brownies that pop—" I glanced at Ben, looking for a little backup here, but it was clear that at the moment he was too busy thinking to talk.

Which is always a dangerous thing.

"Simple," Ben muttered. "Simple and to the point. That's boring, all right, but you know what would make it a lot less boring?"

"If you sprinkled bacon on top?" I guessed.

"Exacto-mundo!" Ben exclaimed, back

at full volume. "Bacon and chocolate chips! That turns a simple, boring recipe into a classic recipe!" He pounded me on the back. "Mac, you're a genius!"

Aretha and I watched as Ben skipped down the hallway.

"Well, at least you got him to take the pepperoni out," Aretha said.

"At least the brownies won't explode all over the judges," I said.

Aretha and I slapped high fives.

Scientifically speaking, it had been a good day.

chapter fifteen

Here are some helpful hints when it comes to making exploding green waffles:

1. Spread newspapers over the kitchen counters and the floor. Like, three days' worth of newspapers. And I mean, put them everywhere. You will be amazed by how far exploding waffle batter can travel.

2. If you get green food coloring on your hands, you will have green hands for at least three days, even if you wash them a hundred times. Believe me, I know.

3. The best thing about exploding waffles is watching them explode.

4. After your waffles explode, you will not be tempted to eat them.

5. Your supervising adult should be the sort of person who's very relaxed and easygoing. It might also be good if they're taking a nap while you're making the waffles.

Fortunately, our supervising adult was Mrs. Klausenheimer. After she showed us how to use the waffle iron and warned us approximately six million times not to burn ourselves, she took her usual place on the couch and pulled a copy of *Celebrity Dogs and Race Cars* from her purse. She yelled, "You kids be careful in there!" every few minutes, but other than that, she pretty much left us alone.

Waffles, in case you're wondering, are really easy to make. Actually, one thing I've learned from all this cooking stuff? Almost everything is really easy to make. You just have to have good directions, and you have to follow them. I mean, okay, baked Alaska probably isn't easy, but other stuff? You'd be surprised.

Anyway, waffle batter is pretty basic: flour, eggs, milk, salt, vegetable oil, and baking powder. Exploding green waffle batter is pretty much the same, only add a bunch of green food coloring and triple the baking powder.

And then stand back.

"All right, folks, this is the big moment, what we've all been waiting for," Ben said as he circled me and Aretha with his video camera, and then pulled in for a close-up of the waffle maker. "Mac and Aretha have carefully mixed together the ingredients for the world's most delicious—and most explosive—waffles. Now watch closely as Aretha carefully pours the batter onto the hot waffle iron. . . . Yes! The batter is on the iron! Aretha slowly pulls down the lid. . . . Now wait for it . . . wait for it . . ."

We waited. And waited. And kept waiting.

Ben checked his watch. "Should it be taking this long?"

"I don't know," Aretha said. "I've never tried exploding waffles before."

Just when I thought nothing was going

to happen, three things happened at the same time:

1. Killer burst through the front door, pulling Evan Forbes along with him.
2. Mrs. Klausenheimer snored the loudest snore ever recorded in human history. In fact, it was so loud that Killer started barking like crazy, Evan yelled like somebody had tackled him from behind, and Ben jumped a mile high and dropped his camera.
3. Which is too bad, because approximately two seconds later, the waffles exploded.

You know that thing I said before about putting newspapers on the counters and the floor?

Well, we didn't actually do that.

Which was too bad, because exploding waffles make a humongous mess.

Maybe you're imagining waffles exploding sort of being like popcorn popping. That's the wrong thing to imagine. First of all, exploding waffles don't wait until they're fully baked to explode. Exploding waffles are half-baked waffles. Another word for half-baked waffles is lava waffles. Okay, "lava waffles" is two words, but you get my point. Visualize lava pouring out of a volcano. It flows like a river. It flows over everything. It covers the floor.

That's your exploding waffle in a nutshell.

Here's something interesting I learned today: German shepherds love exploding green waffles. How did I learn this?

Guess.

When we saw what a mess the exploding waffles were making, everybody started yelling, "Get the paper towels!" and "Get a mop!" What we should have been yelling was "Get Killer!"

As soon as he sniffed that something was up, Killer was in the kitchen. From the look in his eyes, you would have sworn he'd spent all his life dreaming of the day he'd find a kitchen filled with green, half-baked waffle batter. You could practically see him licking his lips.

And then he was licking waffle batter. He licked it off the floor and then he stood up on his hind legs and was licking it off the counters. By this time, Ben had picked up his camera, so of course he was filming. "This is definitely going on YouTube!" he kept yelling. "It's gonna go viral!"

Evan stood in the kitchen doorway and said, "If this is what's for dinner, I'm going to McDonald's."

Aretha was grinning from ear to ear. "The Girl Scouts will never forget this. I'm going to be a legend."

"Maybe you should only double the baking powder when you do this for your troop," I suggested.

"Are you kidding? I'm going to quadruple it! I'm going to make waffles that fly out the windows."

After Killer had filled up on exploded green waffles, everybody cleaned up what was left, even Evan.

I think Killer was having a good influence on him.

Sarah Fortemeyer came at five to give me and Aretha a ride home. After she dropped off Aretha, Sarah looked at me and asked, "Are you feeling okay?"

"I feel great," I told her. "We just did an amazing experiment. The cool thing is, I came up with a hypothesis—that tripling the amount of baking powder in the waffle batter would make the waffles explode—and I was totally right. That's a really big deal for a scientist."

"That's great, Mac," Sarah said. "Only, you're looking a little green."

I looked green for the next three days. Nobody teased me, though.

Evan Forbes wouldn't let them.

It's been weird having Evan Forbes for a friend, but it's not all bad. First of all, Ben and I are training him not to throw his milk cartons at people's heads at lunch, so we're practically the most popular kids in the fourth grade. Secondly, if you need someone to test out brownie recipes on, Evan is definitely your man. He can eat two dozen without even blinking. Or burping, which is even more impressive.

The day before the recipe contest deadline, me, Ben, Aretha, and Evan had a vote. It was between pizza

brownies made with maraschino cherries, marshmallows, and M&M's, and
frosted brownies sprinkled with bacon
and chocolate chips.

The bacon and chocolate chips won
hands down.

Unfortunately, our recipe didn't.

Ben was bummed, but he got over
it. For one thing, his exploding waffles
video has gotten forty-nine hits on You-
Tube, which is forty-eight more than
his last video did. For another thing,
he's gained five pounds from eating
brownies.

In Ben's opinion, genius artists should
be on the chubby side.

Speaking of five pounds, my mom has
lost five pounds since I started cooking.
I guess I could take that as an insult,
except she eats everything I put in front
of her. Now that we only have pizza

once a week, she eats a lot more baked chicken and salad.

Okay, and the occasional bowl of Cheerios.

Hey, I'm a scientist. I can't be cooking up huge feasts all the time.

I've got work to do.

ACKNOWLEDGEMENTS

The author would like to thank the most fabulous Caitlyn Dlouhy and the most marvelous Ariel Colletti for being utterly fabulous and marvelous, and she wants to give a big tip of the hat to Lyn Streck, science teacher extraordinaire. Thanks to Kaitlin Severini, pretty much the best copy editor ever, and to Sonia Chaghatzbanian, the most marvelous book designer. Thank you to the fantastic Laura Ferguson for all of her fantastic work, and lots of love and gratitude to the usual gang of family and friends who keep the author centered and sane, which is no easy job.

Turn the page for a look at another book
in the Phineas L. MacGuire series,

PHINEAS L. MACGUIRE . . . gETS
SLiMED!

FRANCES O'ROARK DOWELL

FROM THE HIGHLY SCIENTIFIC NOTEBOOKS
OF PHINEAS L. MACGUIRE

Phineas L. MacGuire . . . gETS
SLiMED!

My name is Phineas Listerman MacGuire.

Most people call me Mac.

My Sunday-school teacher and my pediatrician call me Phineas.

A few people, mostly my great-uncle Phil and his cockatiel, Sparky, call me Phin.

Nobody calls me Listerman.

Nobody.

I mean not one single person.

Everybody got that?

I am currently in the fourth grade at Woodbrook Elementary School. On the first day of school my teacher, Mrs. Tuttle, asked us to write down our number one, two, and three goals for the year. Here is what I wrote:

1. To be the best fourth-grade scientist ever
2. To be the best fourth-grade scientist ever
3. To be the best fourth-grade scientist ever

So far this has not happened.

For example, I did not win the fourth-grade science fair. Me and my best friend, Ben, got an honorable mention.

We made a volcano. It was a pretty good volcano, since I am an expert volcano maker. But these days it takes more than baking soda and vinegar to get a science fair judge excited.

I learned that the hard way.

Today Mrs. Tuttle asked us to take out our goal sheets and review our goals. She says the first week of November is a good time for goal reviewing. She also says most people who don't meet their goals fail because they forget what their goals were in the first place.

"What is one step you can make this week that will help you meet one of your

goals?" Mrs. Tuttle asked. She took a yellow rubber frog from the jar of rubber frogs she keeps on her desk and balanced it on the tip of her finger. "Think of one small thing you can do."

I put my head down on my desk. After getting an honorable mention in the science fair, the only step I could take was to erase my three goals and start over. Maybe my goal could be to remember to take my gym clothes home on Friday afternoons.

Not that I would ever meet that goal either.

Aretha Timmons, who sits behind me in Mrs. Tuttle's class and who won second place in the fourth-grade science fair, popped her pencil against the back of my head.

"Why so glum, chum?" she asked.

"What goals did you put down, anyway?"

I held up my paper so she could read it. "Hmmm," she said. "Well, it's still pretty early in the year. You could do something amazing before Christmas if you put your mind to it."

Ben, who sits one row over and two seats back from me, leaned toward us. "I've got two words for you, Mac: Albert 'Mr. Genius Scientist' Einstein."

"That's five words," I said.

Maybe Ben's goal should be to learn how to count.

"My point is, Albert Einstein, the most

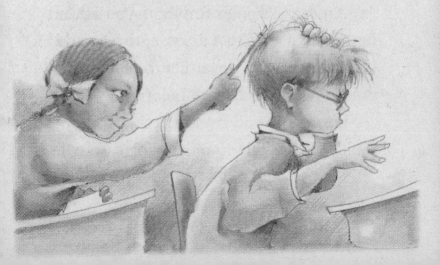

famous genius scientist of the world, flunked math about a thousand times. I don't think he even graduated from high school. He was a complete birdbrain until he was thirty or something."

"I didn't flunk math," I told him. "I just didn't win first prize at the science fair."

"See!" Ben shouted gleefully. "You're even smarter than Albert Einstein."

Ben is not a famous genius scientist, in case you were wondering.

He's a pretty good friend, though.

"What you need is a good project," Aretha said. "For example, if you could figure out a cure to a disease, that would be excellent. I've never heard of a fourth grader curing a disease before."

"Or maybe you could rid the world of mold," Ben said. "I mean, for a fourth grader, you sure know a lot about moldy junk."

It's true. I have always been sort of a genius when it comes to mold. Mold is like science that's happening all over your house, unless your family is really neat and tidy and cleans out the refrigerator on a regular basis.

This does not describe my family at all.

"Not all mold is bad," I told Ben, showing off my geniosity. "In fact, one of the most important medicines ever, penicillin, is made from mold."

"So figure out how to get rid of the bad mold," Ben said. "My mom would give you twenty bucks if you could get rid of the mold in our shower. That's all she ever talks about practically."

Rid the world of bad mold. It sounded

like the sort of thing a superhero would do in a comic book, if comic books were written by scientists with a special interest in single-celled organisms made out of fungus.

I could be Anti-Mold Man, Destroyer of Slime.

Not bad for a fourth grader.

I raised my hand. "Mrs. Tuttle, is it okay to change our goals, at least a little?"

"Revising your goals is a part of the process," Mrs. Tuttle said. "Sometimes we make goals that are unrealistic or not what we really want after all."

"Great!" I took out my pencil and started erasing my number one, two, and three goals. When I was done erasing, I wrote:

1. To get rid of all unnecessary mold in Woodbrook Elementary School
2. To teach Ben how to count
3. To be the best fourth-grade scientist ever

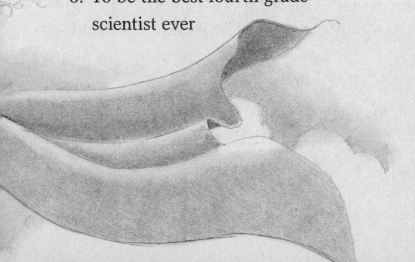

Here is my routine after school is over: First I get off the bus and drag my backpack two blocks down the street to my house, which is located at 2505 Apple Blossom Road. The whole time I'm dragging my backpack, I'm thinking about what a dumb name Apple Blossom Road is, since not only are there no apple trees on my street, there are no other trees with blossoms either.

In fact, there are only seven trees on my street, and they are all oak trees.

The next street after my street is Cherry Tree Lane. Guess how many cherry trees there are?

I have no idea who thinks up this stuff.

After I finally get home, I open my front door and tiptoe to the kitchen, in case my sister, Margaret, who is two, is taking a nap. The last thing I want to do is to wake up Margaret, whose favorite

game is trying to fit her dolls' clothes over my head.

In case you were wondering, this is a very annoying game.

If it were up to me, I would go straight to my room the second I got home. My room is very comfortable. There are clothes everywhere, which gives it the lived-in look. I keep snacks in my underwear drawer and my top desk drawer, usually graham stick packs, snack-size potato chip bags, and chocolate pudding cups. My complete set of the Mysteries of Planet Zindar series is piled up next to my bed, so entertainment is not a problem.

In fact, I'm pretty sure if everyone else on the planet except me got sucked into a black hole, I could stay in my room and be fine for at least four months.

But I am not allowed to go straight to my room. There is a list of rules and regulations posted on our refrigerator, and under "After School," in the number one spot, is "Check in." So when I get home, I go to the kitchen, where I come face-to-face with the worst part of my day.

Her name is Sarah Fortemeyer.

She is the Babysitter from Outer Space.

Now, you would think, me being a scientist and everything, that I would like a space alien for a babysitter. Only, Sarah Fortemeyer is not the good kind of space alien—the kind who could tell you interesting facts about life on Mars, or who could give you lessons in advanced space alien laser beam technology.

No. She is a Teenage Girl Space Alien from the Planet of Really Pink Stuff.

"Hey, Macky Mac," she said the minute I walked into the kitchen today, the same way she does every day. "Ready for your snacky snack?"

I sighed. As a rule, I do not like sentences that rhyme.

Especially when Sarah Fortemeyer says them.

Sarah got up from the kitchen table and began waving her fingers in the air. For a second I thought she was trying to put some Teenage Girl Space Alien spell

on me, but then I noticed the bottles of nail polish on the table.

"What do you think?" Sarah said, coming closer, her fingers still fluttering around. "Today I did three different colors: Ravishing Raspberry, Simply Summer Strawberry, and Green Day Green."

"No comment," I said.

I am a scientist. I do not have opinions on fingernail polish.